The Disturbed

The Disturbed

Shawna Mccallister

Copyright © 2018 by Shawna Mccallister
THE DISTURBED
by Shawna Mccallister

Printed in the USA
ISBN-13: 9781548544300
ISBN-10: 1548544302

Library of Congress Control Number: 2017914703
CreateSpace Independent Publishing Platform
North Charleston, South Carolina

All rights reserved solely by the author. The author guarantees all contents are original and do not infringe upon the legal rights of any other person or persons work. No part of this book may be reproduced or transmitted in any form or by any means, electronic, photocopy, recording, or otherwise, without the prior written permission of the author. The views expressed in this book are not necessarily those of the publisher.

About the Author

Shawna Mccallister was born in Los Angeles, California, and has a background in Psychology. She is the author of "Does Anyone Really Know Me?" "Blinded by Love" "Never Ashamed Never Alone"with her latest two releases being a children's book titled "Bean Learns How to Scoot Scoot" Learning Safety with Bean, and "How Bean Learns Outlet and Plug Safety" Learning Safety with Bean. Mccallister, hopes to turn the tide by providing readers with the tools necessary to triumph over overwhelming trials through positive reading material, as well as find enjoyment within her romance and psychological thriller side of writing. In a couple of her books she does share her own story, biblical inspiration, and a step-by-step guide to daily lifestyle practices designed to help troubled readers cope. Mccallister, shows there's light at the end of the tunnel, no matter how deep, and dark it might seem. With her newly released novel, "The Disturbed" she plans to thrill the socks off *her readers who so dare to read her psychological thriller alone. Also, be looking for some more amazing children's books coming out soon, as well as more thrillers, fantasy, and romance. You can also find "Blinded by Love" for the sexier side of your reading tastes. The children's books she has out as well as the new one's coming out are not only guided towards parents helping their children learn how to read but can be used as tools in being proactive when it comes to their safety with the character named Bean. They can all be found on Amazon.com.*

Shawna Mccallister, is an anointed author of many books, which bring insight to overcoming life's trials, bringing inspiration to hurting individuals, and showing the many talents she has writing in many different genres. She enjoys writing romance, poetry, short stories, psychological thrillers, fantasy, self-help, and children's books with interests in fiction and non-fiction. With a strong desire to have her novels become movies, you'll be seeing a lot more of her very soon.

http://touchedbyabook.wordpress.com
https://www.goodreads.com/Touchedbyabook
Follow Shawna on Twitter @Touchedbyabook
Contact: Authorinfo@Touchedbyabook.com

Author Notes

"*The Disturbed" is thrilling, romantically sexy, and full of chilling suspense.*

Derek has had a history of delusions, which have recently returned. After months of struggling, Derek's friends are seriously wondering if he has gone completely mad. A man begins to follow Derek, but he can't determine if this man is real, or one of his delusions. Derek plans to move to Alabama with his best friend Jazz, leaving the city life behind him, hopeful it will reduce his delusions, only to find he is still being followed.

After moving to Alabama, Derek resumes college life, begins seeing a new therapist, and gets a side job working at a gas station. Derek finds true love in Alabama, but it comes with a cost. He almost loses everything including his life but the one thing that remains strong is his true love. Though no one believes him but the girl he loves as he fights desperately to figure out what is true in his life. Looking into the face of terror, he learns to fight for what's most important and what's most in jeopardy. Will he conquer the hell that's been unleashed in his life in order to get to the heavenly life he so longs for? Don't you hate a tease? You must read the book to find out what happens...

Dare to read alone!

On a more serious note I wanted to mention some things that were heavy on my heart as I wrote this story, and still are. There are many individuals who struggle with mental disorders every day just like Derek. This book was based on a true delusion, and while many see those who have disorders as different or dangerous, this is not always the case, as you will find in Derek's story. Managing disorders can be very difficult and can take a lot of love for the individuals who struggle with any type of mental disorder. Managing takes a lot of love from family and friends who may not understand what causes their underlining behaviors. Many struggle with depression, bipolar, schizophrenia, personality disorders, as well as anxiety, which I believe is the root cause of many of these disorders. It's time to take the stigma off these disorders and for us to realize psychological disorders do not change who we are inside, nor what we can become, they are simply something we have to manage. Sometimes medications, therapy, and meditations can be a big help in doing so. Let's face it; we all have had days that are bad or not so good. We all have been depressed at some point in our lifetimes, but that was not who we were, just how we felt, and

The Disturbed

oftentimes our experiences and circumstance play a role in this and our view of overcoming it. Derek never gave up, not matter how hard shit got for him. All I'm saying is manage your disorders, but never let them define you; let them make you, as well as those around you, better and stronger. Remember this, you are not your disorder, it is only something you must learn to manage. There are resources at the end of this book, in the event you may need them or know someone who would. Enjoy reading.
Best Regards,
Shawna Mccallister

Contents

About the Author · · · · · · · · · · · · · · ·v
Author Notes · · · · · · · · · · · · · · · · ·vii

Chapter 1 Following · 1
Chapter 2 Change in Plans · · · · · · · · · · · · · · · 13
Chapter 3 The Fishing Trip · · · · · · · · · · · · · · 23
Chapter 4 Need for Change · · · · · · · · · · · · · · 45
Chapter 5 Finding True Love · · · · · · · · · · · · · 71
Chapter 6 Disturbed · · · · · · · · · · · · · · · · · · · 113
Chapter 7 Call for Back-up · · · · · · · · · · · · · · 143
Chapter 8 Delusion or Truth · · · · · · · · · · · · · 175
Chapter 9 Going Home · · · · · · · · · · · · · · · · · 203
Chapter 10 Heaven and Hell · · · · · · · · · · · · · · 225
Chapter 11 Truth Exposed · · · · · · · · · · · · · · · 245

Resources ·287

CHAPTER 1

Following

My name is Derek Holson and this is my story as I remember it. I guess you can say I'm a jack-of-all-trades. I am not your typical guy. I mean, I'm tall, dark and handsome mostly from my Italian breeding, but I am a far cry from your average dude. It's true we all have struggles, but to say the least of my struggles have been in my head, would be an understatement. I mean, wondering what was real from what wasn't in many seasons of my life, sure made me question everything that much more. You see, when I was fifteen I was diagnosed with anxiety, manic depression, and bipolar. I also had delusions once in a while or at least what I thought were delusions, which really sucked because I really felt different from everyone else at school. Talk about a rough teenage life, man rough was not even close to how I saw shit. I grew up in Los Angeles, California, that's where I lived most of my life, until my parents bought a home up in Big Bear, which moved us pretty much out of the city. Although I still had to commute back and forth every day, my life felt like a fucking delusion most of the time.

I had been in college four years, and had just graduated from CSU, which was a nice drive from home on my attending days. My G.P.A. was 3.44 almost a 4.0, not too bad for a guy with disorders, at least I had no complaints; I mean, I had some smarts. But during the last semester of college I started to experience more delusions, which I had not had in many years. The hardest part was I could not tell the difference between some of the real events of my life from the made-up ones in my head. To tell you the truth, that shit can be pretty scary not to mention frustrating. My parents were always very supportive, and I was grateful for that, but I struggled with the thoughts of why I had to be born so different. I struggled with the fact that I could not control my thoughts sometimes, which oftentimes pissed me off. It was also hard on my relationships over the years. I had trouble at school growing up because if people got close enough to know me

The Disturbed

they would also find out I had to take medication for my stupid ass disorders, and this gave me a complex for sure. I hated being different. I hated how people viewed me. I hated how the meds affect my moods and how my disorders affect my life.

During the last three years, I had seemed to whip my disorders in the ass, so to speak until this last semester in college. I was still seeing a therapist, as I had for years, and was not sure what brought it on again, but shit started happening and it cost me a relationship with a girl I really liked. Okay, somewhat liked. But as it seemed she was not the right one anyway, as mom would also remind me. I started having delusions again, but they were different than before. These delusions seemed so damn real, so much so that I was arguing with my therapist, girlfriend, and parents because my inner thoughts were so loud, and determined. It was as if something evil wanted to destroy my life. Not only that, but for a guy that sure doesn't scare easily, I was fucking scared! I kept seeing this man appear out of fucking nowhere. The fucked-up part about it was that, although, I had all this support in my life, surrounding me, so called trying to help me, I was so fucking alone. I could not explain what it was I was seeing but he, "it" sure the hell was not like any normal looking man. This manly looking thing was all white and seemed to have no face at all, only indents where his eyes would be and a nose with no nostrils, lips with no opening. A man but not a man, more like a mannequin! He was tall and wore a black jacket when I saw him appear most of the time and a white flannel shirt underneath it. When I thought about the delusions I would wonder how the fuck he could breathe if he was real. He never spoke but would show up out of nowhere. If I was in the bathroom getting ready for school, I would look up to check my face for toothpaste and bam! There he was behind me in the fucking mirror! The faceless fuck, the jacket, the smirk. It was like I was seeing a ghostly mannequin with the outlines of a face, but no realness to it. All I could make out was the smirk, and the deep eyes, but all I saw in them was darkness. The darkness felt real, but I couldn't tell if the evil eyes were part of this faceless fuck, or a complete delusion. When I went to turn around again after looking away there was no one there, but me. I always felt the hair on my neck stand up as if there was an eerie presence of something in the room, or wherever I was during the encounters.

There was this one particular night I had been out with friends and decided to walk home. It was a full moon night and the street lights were just coming on. As I walk down this lamp lit street alone I had a very eerie feeling, as if I was being watched or followed. Whenever I would

The Disturbed

struggle with anxiety or delusions I would always turn on my music to try and distract myself from what was really happening or how I was really feeling. But this particular night that didn't work.

As I walked down the dark street a song came on that a friend had told me someone she knew had committed suicide to. Well that sure the hell didn't help walking alone down this shitty street. Then all of a sudden in the middle of this song my iPod shut off. After that happened I began to walk a lot faster because I had no fucking distraction at all from what had just happened. My walk turned into a speed-walk now, I was so fucking spooked. I looked up, and could see the full moon right in front of me. It looked huge, as if the damn thing had grown as I walked. I stared at the moon hoping for some relief, but shit got worse. The street lights started to flicker, then I saw him. Hiding behind a bush he stuck his head out first, then his whole body. I crossed the street as my pace almost became a run. I could not help but look back, but tried to pretend as if I was looking for traffic, hoping he would think I hadn't noticed him at all. He stood there a minute, then was gone. Then suddenly my iPod turned back on. The lights on the street stopped flickering as I came to the last block on the street which, seemed to take forever. Well, after that night I started to see my therapist more often just to feel

5

a bit okay and have some type of an outlet. I guess you can say it was kind of a breaking point, as far as making some much need changes in my life. When I tried to explain what had happened to my then girlfriend Becky, she straight out told me she was done hearing about my stories, stalkers and villains. I think she was cheating on me too because she had been acting different for a few weeks, I just could not put my finger on why. Needless to say, we broke-up but at the time for me it was kind of a relief. She was kind of a bitch anyway and never really seemed to care about the real me, nor was she supportive of me managing my issues. Becky, most of the time, complained about how I was not measuring up in one way or another. And her god-awful primping and perfume made me want to gag half the time because she about bathed in it.

After graduation and the bad breakup with Becky, I did some much-needed soul-searching and I decided to make some life changing decisions. Although I pretty much had my mind set on what I planned to do and what I wanted to change, I felt I should at least talk to the important people in my life, and my therapist, about the decisions I was contemplating. I had a talk with my parents about my desire to move away to the country where it was a bit slower and finishing up my graduate degree there. They thought it'd be a good idea to make an appointment with Dr. Searian, my

The Disturbed

therapist before I committed completely to the idea. I also wanted to see if it would help with the delusions I had been experiencing wondering if the stresses of the last few months had influenced me falling back into having the delusions in the first place.

My appointment with Dr. Searian was tomorrow afternoon and I was sure hoping she would agree with my plans I had given a lot of thought too. I was a bit nervous on my way to my appointment. It was time to get some input from my therapist and see what she thought about my changing environments, and if she agreed it would benefit me to have a change in scenery, or if she thought I was running away from my problems instead of facing them. I walk into the lobby of Dr. Searian's office and was greeted by her receptionist, who I had a crush on. Her name was Katy, and she had the sexiest voice. Even when I would call to make my appointments I found myself not wanting to get off the phone. I could listen to her talk all damn day and look at her too. Her long tan legs, red hair, and glasses teased my school-boy fetish for sure.

"Good afternoon, have a seat, Dr. Searian is in session but will be with you shortly."

"Sure. Thank you."

As I sat there looking around the office I truly wondered how I had gotten here. Not to the office, but why I was at the office to begin with. I knew I was smart,

educated, raised well, and yet I felt so different and sometimes alone in my differences. On the outside, people that just met me couldn't tell I had a psychological disorder or struggle at all. Hell, I was not even sure what the fuck I was dealing with either, but I sure struggled with some crazy crap.
"Dr. Searian will see you now."
I got up and headed towards her office. She stood and walked over to greet me as I shut the door.
"Hello Derek, a pleasure to meet with you again, have a seat."
"Hello Dr. Searian, yeah, glad I could get an appointment so soon. Thanks for seeing me."
"So, tell me, how have things been going?"

"Well, to be honest, not so good the last couple of months. Ever since last semester started I guess. I started having these strange delusions again, but now they seem so real. I mean, before I would have thoughts of things that many times were not true, but now I'm seeing things that seem too real, and feel to real. It's caused me to lose my girlfriend, and other people in my life because they just don't want to be around me anymore. I guess they think I am crazy or got some screws loose up there, but Dr. Searian something is seriously happening to me and around me. When I try and explain it to people I know who are supposed to care about me, instead of supporting me they don't want to hear it anymore. But what I am going through makes no sense and I can't say I blame them much. This has to be real, it can't just be in my head, but I just don't have any damn proof that it's real, not even for myself."

"Derek, why don't you explain to me briefly what's happening."

"Well, I keep seeing this man, at least I think it's a man, but he has no face. He has features of a man but not a real man with eyes or normal features. He's white and the best way I can describe him is that he looks something like a mannequin. That's about the best description I can give but he follows me and pops out of crazy places. I've even seen him while I was brushing my teeth in the mirror. I looked in the mirror to check my mouth for toothpaste and he was right behind me. It scared the crap out of me. But when I turn around, no one was in the room. Doc! Am I going crazy here?"

"Derek, I would not say you are going crazy but you could possibly be experiencing delusions again and possibly be under too much stress. Remember when we spoke last, I had told you that there is always a possibility that the delusions could return, especially if you stopped taking the medication I prescribed. I would suggest making some changes in your schedule and make sure you are getting enough rest. How's your sleep?"

"My sleep has been about the same except for finals and last semester's crunch. I guess I have been a bit sleep deprived. However, there are a few things I wanted to talk to you about.

"After this last semester ended, and my girlfriend and I broke up, the delusions started up again. I did a lot of thinking about myself, my future, and what I want for my life. I was thinking about getting out of the city. Maybe move to the country, find a nice college in Alabama, and see if the slower pace would help me get my brain functioning right again. To be honest doc this delusion stuff is getting to me and it's getting old, not to mention what it's doing to my life."

"Well Derek, it's good you are taking time to manage your disorder and making healthy changes to your lifestyle. In fact, as much as I would hate to see you move, I believe it is important for you to be in a less stressed environment and I see no issues with your new goals. However, I do suggest you find a good therapist when you get to where you plan on moving to, and I think it would be a good idea to take the medication I prescribed you."

"Well, I have to agree with you there doc, even though I hate taking pills, it's worth a shot."

"Good to hear Derek. I'm glad you agree to at least try the medication to see if it will help any. Also Derek, make sure you inform your new therapist of all medications you are taking and I'll have your medical files transferred so they will be more familiar with you and what we have discussed during our sessions. This will help them better understand what we have worked on in our sessions. This will also give them a place to start with you, so you can continue managing the very best way possible. Do you have an idea about where you want to move or do you have a date planned?"

"Well, I would like to move soon. I have been talking with my parents about my plans to move for a couple of months now. I was thinking about moving to Alabama, and continuing my education at Alabama State University. Get a part-time job to help with living expenses and it's something to get me out of the house apart from just going to college. I just feel like it's time for a change. You know?"

"Sounds like you have a great plan in order, and you have been giving it a lot of thought as well Derek. If you'd like to meet again before you move please be sure to call to schedule another appointment before you go, otherwise I wish you the very best Derek, you have made some great progress. Please be sure to take your medications and let me know if there is anything else I can do between now and when you do set out on your new amazing journey."

"Thank you Dr. Searian, I appreciate your time, and you not making me feel like a complete "nut-case." I will keep in touch." I get up from my seat at the same time she does, we shake hands, and off I go, feeling a bit relieved it seems with her blessing on my plans to move.

I get to my car and sit there a minute thinking out-loud to myself, 'Well, I guess I am moving.' Now I have to convince my friend Jazz to go with me. Shouldn't be too hard, I mean we have been best friends since grade school. His name is Jazz Kingston and if there's anyone that knows me on the planet, it's Jazz. In fact, he knows me even better than my therapist.

CHAPTER 2

Change in Plans

Derek

I tried calling Jazz after leaving therapy, feeling anxious to ask, but I really wanted to make sure he was committed to going with me to Alabama. I mean we had talked about it before but not in detail. He didn't answer so I decided to just go talk to him about it.

I get to the house and knock on Jazz's door; his younger sister comes to the door. "Hey Krista, is Jazz home?"

"Yep but it will cost you a quarter to come in!" She says in her cute little munchkin voice.

"A whole quarter? Aww man, let me see what I got. Oh Yeah!" I shout with excitement showing her the quarter as I pull it from my pocket.

"Yay," she shouts as she jumps up and down yelling for Jazz to come to the door, and opening it all the way now, summoning me to come in.

I see Jazz come down the stairs as he stares at Krista's excitement, confused as to what she was up to now. "She'll be okay, she's just expressing her pure joy over the quarter she earned for my meeting with you." I smile at him jokingly.

"Well, I wasn't allowed in without the payment."

"Krista!" Jazz says sternly.

"Don't be charging for people to see me, that's my job little miss." Having fun with her, he tickles her before we both walk upstairs to his room to hangout and discuss what was on my mind of course, the move.

"So, what's up bud?" Jazz says out loud noticing the serious look on my face.

"Well, remember I told you I was going to talk to my therapist about the plans I had to relocate?"

"Yeah, what did she say?"

"She was way supportive, and thought it could be good for me. Buuuttt! I really want you to come with man! I came over to see if you were serious about really going with me, because I am really committed to moving now."

"Well Derek, you have always been my bud, and there is no way I could stay here without my best friend man. No way in hell!"

"So, does that mean you are going?"

"If you're going then I'm going man."

"Fuck yeah! You don't know how much this means to me. This is going to be fucking amazing exploring, and making shit happen on our own. I'm so damn psyched right now dude, you have no clue.

"I'm psyched too man, can't wait to get out of here, and get on the open road."

"Me either. Hey Jazz, make sure you talk to your mom dude; make sure she's cool with you leaving. I'm going to go talk to mine right now, and let them know what the therapist said, and all is a go."

"I'll call you later and we can hangout okay?"

"Yeah man, let's catch a midnight flick or something tonight okay?"

"Sounds good, later dude!"

"Later."

I head out the door of Jazz's house, waving goodbye to Krista as I leave. She waves back and gives a grin as if she knows I have money now and will raise the rate on entry to Jazz next time.

I get in my car and drive home, it's been a long day or it seemed that way anyway. It feels good to finally walk into my house. I see mom in the kitchen and my dad in front of the TV as always. But for some reason I am realizing how much I will miss them. I guess it's because I know I am really moving now, having my mind made up and the fact that they both have been so damn supportive makes it that much harder to leave.

"Hey Mom!"

"Hi Derek, how did the meeting go son?"

"Well, I wanted to talk to you and Dad during dinner if that would be okay."

"Sure son, dinner will be ready in about ten minutes or so."

"Great! Thanks Mom, I am starving."

I go in the other room to say hi to my Dad and make some small talk, just catching up on what Dad's been doing, then wash up for dinner. Hoping my decision to move doesn't shock Mom too much. We talked about it already, but now that this was my final decision I was sure there would be some tears shed for sure.

"Boys dinners ready!" Mom yells out.

"Coming Mom."

We sit down at the dinner table where Mom laid out an awesome meal. Steak, veggies, baked potatoes, I mean

The Disturbed

the works. I think to myself that not only will I miss being here but how much I will miss Moms cooking too.

"So, Derek, how did it go today at your meeting? Don't keep us in suspense."

"It went well Mom. Remember I had expressed to you a few months ago having a desire to move to more of a country surrounding?"

"Yes."

"That's pretty much why I went to talk to her today. Although I have been having some issues in the last few months, I wanted to ask her if getting away from the stress of the city may help me, and much to my relief she said it would or could anyway. Mom, Dad, I have been giving this a lot of thought and I really want to live in a slower paced area, not so busy, or stressful, you know. The thought of leaving here hurts me, but I feel I have to try to see if it helps me at least."

As I share my heart, baring my soul, I see tears in my Mom's eyes and it's killing me to tell them my decision although I know in my heart I must.

Mom stays quiet, struggling not to cry.

"Derek, where have you decided to move? And is this a final decision? Are you going to come back?"

Questions pour out of Mom as Dad cuts his steak as he listens, probably having the same questions as Mom.

"Well, I have planned to move to Alabama, go to Alabama State University to finish college and finish my Master's degree there. Jazz is also going with me. Mom, I know this seems like a big leap, but I think I am ready and the therapist said she thinks it could be really good for me."

"Derek you know me and your father want the very best for you, so if this is what will make you happy, yes son, you have to at least try. But you must visit on as many holidays as possible please because we will miss you deeply around here"

"Aww Mom, Dad you know I will always visit every chance I get."

"We are proud of you Derek." Dad says, and as my heart warms I feel tears in my eyes now and a lump in my throat as I swallowed hard trying to keep back the flood of emotions I was feeling.

"Thank you Dad, thank you Mom, for your support and for being the best parents a kid could ever imagine."

We all smile at each other and finish dinner.

"Hey Derek, I want to get a fishing trip in before you leave if that's alright with you son."

"Sure Dad, I would like that very much."

"You busy next weekend?"

"Nope, we will just be getting all our paperwork and packing ready so we will be here for about two more weeks."

"Sounds great, then next weekend it is."

The Disturbed

"Sweet looking forward to it, Pops."

Mom smiles big and looks at Dad and I knowing this will be a special trip indeed.

I called Jazz back and told him I was going to stay in and give him more time to talk to his family as well instead of hitting the movies like we had planned.

I watch a bit of TV with Dad then go to my room for the night.

Getting ready to crash I remember Dr. Searian wanted me to stay on those meds she prescribed. Although I didn't want to start them again, I took her advice anyway hoping for some relief from those damn delusions. I took the pill and hopped into bed thinking about the day and all the hopes I have for my adventurous move. So many emotions flood my heart and mind, but I know it will all work itself out. Laying there I jot down a few notes of errands I have to get done before Jazz and I leave. Putting the pen and paper down on the nightstand, I feel the effects of the medication kick in and I am off to sleep.

Morning comes, and Mom knocks lightly on the door to my bedroom.

"Derek? You up? I made pancakes, eggs, and bacon."

"Yeah, Mom, be down in a minute."

As I rub my eyes trying to shake off my sleepiness. I can smell fresh brewed coffee and bacon as the aroma traveled all the way upstairs to my room. I wash up really quick, and fly down the stairs.

Mom really made an amazing breakfast and part of me knows it's because I am leaving, but I think none of us wanted to discuss any of that anymore until after the weekend at least. I had a big trip with Dad planned for this weekend but I really wanted to make some time for Mom as well. She had always been the one to keep the family together when things got hard and made everything seem alright even when it wasn't sometimes.

Dad was the hard-ass most of the time, and Mom, I guess, learned to just take it and make the best of it. I hated seeing Dad take shit out on Mom when he had a hard day or came home in a bad mood. Mom always greeted him with love, and seemed to know just what to do to soothe Dad and me when we were lost in our own struggles. Mom always kept me stable as well, I mean there were days I really was afraid of my own-self and Mom had the right words to say every time. She has been the heart and soul of the family and I know I will feel lost without her for a while after I leave. Even the phone will not be the same as having her there in the next room. It will be one of the hardest things for me to do I am sure, but I do have to spend some one on one time with Mom too. Let her know what she has meant to me all of these

The Disturbed

years and how much I have appreciated all she has done for me. Time to grow-up Derek and have that talk with Mom soon. I realize I am schooling myself as I get ready to leave. I must grow-up sometime no matter how hard it may seem at the time of the lesson.

CHAPTER 3

The Fishing Trip

It was finally time for Dad and I to go on our weekend fishing trip, and I couldn't wait to get on the road. We have not been fishing for a few years and I know Dad sure needs some time away from the monotony of the same every day routine of work and home, not to mention his TV watching. We wake early Saturday morning, grab a quick bite to eat, and load up Dad's truck to get ready to head to the lake cabin. Dad and Mom have owned the cabin for years now, although we have not been down there much in the last few years. I guess mainly Dad just hasn't had the time, nor had I for the last couple of years. Today should prove to be an awesome experience which, I will treasure forever I am sure. I had thought about asking Jazz to tag along, but I wanted this day to be special. Just Dad and I, and I think Dad had the same thing in mind as well.

Truck loaded, gassed up, off we go. The lake is about an hour away so it gave Dad and me time to catch-up an shoot the breeze.

"So, Dad how long has it been since we have been down to the lake anyway?"

"Humm, have to say almost three years now, huh?"

Yeah, I think that sounds about right.

"Why don't you and Mom ever take a getaway to the cabin?"

"Oh, I guess your mother is not the rough-it, outdoorsy type as much anymore.

We've pretty much become homebodies" Dad says with a chuckle.

"So, you excited about moving son?"

"Yeah, a bit nervous too, I guess. I won't have you and Mom there. I mean moving so far away and being on my own is pretty scary. But at the same time, I am hoping new surroundings, and a fresh start may help my thinking you know, and my disorder anyway."

"Well son, always know that your mother and I are just a phone call away and you are always welcome back if you get homesick." Dad says with a big grin as if he hopes I will come running back home.

At the Cabin
We arrive at the cabin and step out of the truck.
"She sure looks like she could use some love, huh?"
It's been so long since we invested any paint or did much cleaning up here. But she's still a beaut.
"I have to agree with you there Dad, and nothing beats the sunset here." I say as I grab a handful of stuff we packed for our trip.
"Hey son, let me help you with that."

We walk up to the door and as Dad sets the stuff down to unlock the cabin an eerie feeling comes over me, almost as if I am being watched. I don't mention it to Dad because I don't want him to start thinking I am going on one of my mind trips again. I glance around the area feeling the urge to know what is lurking and see nothing. Just let it go Derek and try and have a good time with Dad, I tell myself trying to make my thoughts louder than the eeriness so I can shake it off.

"Hey Dad, what do you say we have some lunch before we head out on the lake?"

"Sounds great to me son."

"Alright, turkey, salami, with swiss laid on a fresh hoagie or rye, Pop?"
"Let's do some hoagies, I'll get the chips and drinks together."
I dust off the table in the kitchen and make our hoagies, and they are amazing, I might add. Dad grabs the chips and sodas and sits down with me.
Both of us being lovers of golf and football we'd be tempted to turn on the TV, but that was one reason Mom insisted there be no TV at the cabin.
Mother knows best.

Dad and I finish our lunch then grab our poles and gear and head to the fishing boat.
We pile everything in the boat.
"Oh shit!" Dad said out loud.
"These damn spiders."
"Hey Derek, head back up to the cabin and get the glass cleaner and some paper towels will yah son? I want to make sure we are not riding along with any more of these bastards."

I start to make my way back up the hill to the cabin which is about 50 feet from where Dad is. I look up to make sure I am headed in the right direction and I see him!

The Disturbed

"Oh fuck! Oh fuck!" I start to panic almost frozen in my steps. I quickly look back at Dad, wanting to yell at him for help but at the same time knowing I can't upset him. Not on our trip. I look back up again and the face or man, whatever I keep seeing, is gone. But I am scared as fuck to go up to the cabin. My thoughts are racing like mad, not knowing if I should walk slow to be on the safe side or rush the fucking cabin ready for a fight. I have been taking my meds; I mean really what the fuck is going on with me? I decide to take the slow pace, but not too slow because now Dad is waiting. Trying to put it in the back of my head, I try and walk as if I saw nothing at all. Scared as fuck, my gut in knots about to puke-up the sandwich I just ate, I reach the cabin stairs. God, I wish I had a gun right now, but I have a small knife on me, I remember as I move out of Dad's view now.

I slowly open the door and walk in the cabin, the door creaks behind me as I head to the sink. Taking a quick look behind me again, I feel relieved there is nothing there. I reach under the sink cabinet grab the glass cleaner, then the paper towels and jet out of the cabin. As I race around the corner of the cabin, I take another glance back and I see him again. This time I look longer wanting so much for this not to be real, then he smirks at me with the outline of his non-existent lips.

I start to run to meet Dad, and almost stumble down the hill. I turn back again and he's gone. My mouth open breathing so fast I can hardly catch my breath as I reach Dad.

"What happened son? Why are you breathing so fast, and what took you so long?"
"Oh, sorry Dad, I almost slid down the hill coming back."

I say to him trying not to alert his suspicions. We finally get out on the water and catch a few fish. After a few hours, we call it a day, having caught more than enough for dinner for the next week. Dad and I fry them up as we settle in for the evening with a nice fire. I am not feeling too cozy after what had happened earlier. I wish I could talk to Dad about it but knowing how much I will miss him after I move I keep silent about it, not wanting to taint our last trip together for a while. I can't help but feel as if I am being watched. I am paranoid that he, or it, is out there still watching our every move.

"Dad I will close all the drapes so the mosquitos don't get in okay?"
"Sure son that's fine with me."

I hated lying to Dad but if I didn't shut them surely, he would catch on to something being wrong with me.

Walking to the side window I reach to pull the drapes shut and I heard a thud on the side of the cabin wall.

"What was that Derek?"
"Not sure Dad? Maybe a pine-shark falling from the trees?"

We've called pine-cones that fall from the pine-trees, 'pine-sharks' ever since I was a little tike running around. Nervous to open the drapes but knowing if I don't Dad may go looking, I open them. There he is staring right at me.

"Auuhh!" I yell at the top of my lungs as I fall back, landing on my ass. "Oh God! Oh God," I say out loud. Dad rises from his chair.

"What in God's green earth is wrong Derek?"
"Sorry Dad, I saw my own reflection in the window and it scared the hell out of me."
"You sure seem pretty jumpy today, you sure you are okay son?"
"Yeah Dad, I am fine. Guess I am not used to being out here as much as I was as a kid."
"Well, if we have as great of a catch tomorrow as we did today, we may head back a day earlier to get these fish stored up. There's not enough room here to store another two days."

"Sounds great to me Dad. We sure did good today didn't we?"

I say, trying to change the subject and fully agree with Dad on heading back a day early.

We both pass-out after sharing amazing stories for a couple of hours. Hope tomorrow will be better than today, at least in my head.

Morning came and as Dad had predicted, we caught so much fish we would have to head back this evening rather than stay another night. Boy was I relieved to know that. I sure loved being here with Dad, but my demons seemed to shatter every bit of fun out of the time at the cabin and I hated it.

We decided to fry up some more fish for a late lunch before we cleaned up and headed home. Damn Dad can cook! Almost as good as Mom, although, I could never tell her that. My mind reflects back over the years as I sit here with Dad listening to one of his amazing stories in this old cabin and eating our catch of the day. For an instant I think to myself, I can't move away from here. I will miss Mom and Dad too much and I have never lived anywhere without them. Insecurities set in as I think of not being able to come home to my room every night as I have for twenty-four years.

"Derek! Are you even listening to my story?"

The Disturbed

"Uh yeah Dad." Shaking my head as if I was coming from a day dream.
"I was just thinking how much I will really miss you and Mom. Well, Mom's cooking too, and my room."
"Oh Derek, your mother and I will miss you very much and will always be here if you need us. I think you have some good things planned. Sometimes it's hard stepping out into the world on your own, but you need to get out and experience life, and the world outside of California. I think you moving to Alabama's a great way to do that son. It's much cheaper too. So there is an added bonus."
I nod and agree with dad. "I guess it's going to be a process of adjustment in many different ways Dad."
Again, Dad was right and it felt great to tell him how I was feeling. In fact, maybe all the anxiety about moving is causing the delusion to come back as well. I thought to myself as the reasoning kicked in to help calm my fretting. I turn on the radio for the rest of the ride home enjoying the view. We reach the house and mom comes outside to greet us.
"How did it go guys?"
"Derek and I brought back damn-near the whole lake of fish"
"I figured you guys must had done good coming back a day early."

Mom grabs some fish and takes it in.

"Looks like fish for a whole month."

"You guys have a good time?"
"We had a blast Mom. You know Dad and his amazing stories always sooth the soul."

I start helping Dad unload the truck.
Just then my phone rings, it's Jazz.
"Got to take this Dad."
"No problem son, I got this."

"Hey Jazz. What's up buddy? We just got back from the cabin right now."
"Not much, just checking on you and seeing if you want to come by later so we can make sure we are ready to roll."
"Alright, sounds good. Let me finish up unloading, get cleaned up and I will swing by your pad, okay?"
"Sounds good, Late."
Jazz hangs up... Late, being short for later, it's always been our guy thing.
Mom comes out of the house.

"Derek? I am planning a get together this Thursday evening for you and Jazz before you guys leave, kind of like a going away party, although this will always be your home son."

Mom says, reassuringly.
"Wow, Mom thanks, sounds great."
"Make sure you and Jazz get here by about seven thirty okay."
"Sure thing mom. We will be here."

Back to Jazz's House

I get to Jazz's house and he and Krista are playing in the yard. We had talked on the phone a few minutes ago so he knew I was on my way.

I get out of the car as Krista comes running up to me to greet me.

"Hey Derek! What you doing here?"

Krista leave Derek alone, he's here to see me.

"Jazz it's cool, at least I am not being charged to meet with you today…"

"Funny!" Jazz, says sarcastically.

We head up the stairs to Jazz's room and both plop down on his futon.

"So, mom has a going away party planned for us on Thursday at about seven thirty. She's requesting your presence as well."

"Oh yeah? Nice I'll go, sounds fun."

"So, what all do you have left to do before we go?"

"Well, I pretty much have the college ready to go as far as transcripts and things being transferred."

"How about you?"

"Yeah, I have everything done and I'm all set to go. And there is what I am bringing in the car or trailer with us." Jazz points to a corner in the room to the things neatly placed in a pile.

"One of the main things we will be doing once we get there is finding a place to stay, but we are manly men we can rough-it until we do, right?"

"Yeah Derek. We got this bro. I ready when you are to hit the road."

"Jazz, how much money you got?"

"I have about close to three grand."

"You?"

"I have about four grand thanks to my parents. So, between the two of us we will be doing great once we get settled there. Make sure you bring shit like your birth certificate and important crap. Okay Jazz? We'll need all that paperwork to be able to change our license and shit like that once we are there."

"Got that covered too Derek."

"Righteous. Then we are set, besides going to mom's sending off party, ha ha ha."

"Sounds like we are good to go. I will miss Krista a lot though." Jazz says with his head a bit low.

The Disturbed

"You know I will too, she is a special smart little girl. But Jazz, we will always come and visit man. It's not like we are never coming back, right? Think of it like a vacation or something only a bit longer."

"What do you say we take her to the movies tonight, we never went the other day."

"Let's go, I am sure she would love that too."

"Nice, let me go tell my mom I am stealing her for a while if she will let me."

We head back down stairs and Jazz gets the go ahead to take Krista with us to the movies. So, we tell her what we are doing and she hops up and down screaming with excitement.

"Goody Goody, let's go!"

Mom yells out, "No rated R! Only G or PG."

"You got it mom!" Jazz yells back.

And we are off to the movies.

About an hour and quarter into the movie Krista falls asleep leaning on Jazz's shoulder. I am sure it is a moment he will not soon forget, especially under the circumstances. I am sure she will treasure it as well.

I drop Jazz and Krista back off at home and drive back to my house, thinking and rethinking if I was forgetting

35

anything before we leave. All of our things will fit in the car and the small trailer we are towing. I guess it's probably because I am feeling so much stress from making such a big step and change in my life. My brain is working over-time right now for sure.

I'm feeling a lot of anxiety as well. On top of everything, considering I am leaving everything and everyone I have ever known except Jazz. But at the same time, I have an excitement about everything being new, starting over in a less stressful environment. I just keep telling myself one day at a time Derek.

It's late when I get home so I just go up to my room, take my meds, and it's off to bed. Going to get a few things like some munchies for our road trip tomorrow, and then get a nap in before mom's shin-dig for Jazz and me.

I get up to my room and I find my window is open. I know mom would not have opened my window and I didn't open it before I left, but as an almost natural reaction now I have that eerie feeling again. I could have sworn it was closed when I left. Well, I will ask mom about it tomorrow as I try and reason with myself to calm down. I sure am glad those meds make me a bit sleepy because I am not sure I could sleep tonight if they didn't.

Just then I get a text from Jazz asking if I got home alright and telling me he had stopped by earlier in the day and I was not home. Must have been when I was with my

The Disturbed

parents checking out trailers for the move. That is odd that Jazz didn't mention that when I was at his house.

I text him back that,

"We had been looking at trailers to fit the hitch earlier today, and no problem, sorry we missed you man, see you tomorrow at the shin-dig."

He texts back,

"Alright have a good night late."

"Late" I text back.

Then I was off to sleep.

Mom and Me Time

I wake in the morning and again my fuckin window is open. I knew I shut it before I went to bed, what the hell? I do my morning routine before flying down the stairs to get some breakfast.

"Morning Mom"

"Good morning, Derek" I made some eggs, bacon, and hot cakes if your hungry son."

"Awesome! Thanks. Hey Mom, did you or dad open my window yesterday or this morning?"

"No son, I haven't been inside your room and your father has been with me the whole time pretty much besides bathroom breaks."

Mom chuckles.

37

Now I am alarmed again. If they didn't open the window then who did and why? I am sure going to make sure its locked tight now.

"Hey Mom, I have to go get some stuff from the store want to go with me?"

"What do you need to get son?"

"I don't know, just something to munch-on the way, some drinks and stuff."

"Yeah, I guess you're right, you boys will be on a trip for a couple of days. Sure son, let me get ready and I'll go with you."

"Great! Thanks Mom."

While mom gets ready, I run upstairs to make sure that damn window is locked because I can't get it out of my head. I grab the list I made, get my shoes on, and I hear Mom yell up at me.

"Derek, I'm ready"

"Coming Mom!"

"I want to stop and get a couple of flannels too because I know the weather is going to be cold." I say as it starts to rain.

We get some shopping done and head to lunch. Mom has a thing for Chinese food, as do I and I wanted some one on one time with her too before I move which is a day and half away now. Time seems to fly by as we reminisce on old special memories and stories which have us both choked up.

The Disturbed

"Derek, do you remember when you were little, how you would always want to help me in the kitchen and how we would go to the senior home down the street and share baked goods we made?"

"Mom, I remember that like it was yesterday."

"Derek, never forget to be a help to those around you son. Those are some very special memories to me." Mom says, as she grabs a tissue from her purse.

"I'll never forget what you and Dad taught me Mom, I promise. I may be moving and changing my address, but one thing is for sure, I'm a Holson inside and out Mom, I have the best parents in the world. Thank you, Mom for raising me with love, and teaching me how to be a man. Dad's a bit harder to say that to, but I am truly grateful for you both."

"Aww, son, you have been our life. Even though you have been grown for a while now, it's still very hard letting go as a parent, ya know. The Mom in me wants to beg you to stay, but I also realize you are older now and have to find your way, what makes you happy. So, I have to be okay with it, but you better visit often or I'll come hunt you down." Mom says, with a squint in her eye.

"I promise Mom, I already want to come visit and I haven't even left yet." I say with a smirk of love.

We continue to talk about old times and special memories, as we finish our lunch, and then hit the 31 Flavors for some ice cream before heading back to the house. Mom has taken me to this place for years. I guess it's kind of both of our ways of holding on to my being young and so carefree, when life as we both know it is about to change. Bitter sweet for sure.

Mom's Going Away Party
We got home and I took in the groceries and flannels I had bought, then I went upstairs to catch a short nap before Mom's shin-dig starts.

Seven o'clock rolls around and it's time to mingle. Not sure who all Mom invited, but I know it will be fun and the food amazing as always knowing how Mom does shin-digs. Just then Jazz runs up the stairs and knocks lightly on my door.

"Hey Derek, you almost done primpin?"

"Hey man, you here already? Cool."

"So, whose all down there?"

"Everyone we know man, almost the whole school, well at least our grad class anyway."

"Nice!"

"Yeah, your Mom really meant a shin-dig too. Lots of food dude. Let's get down there and mingle man."

"I'm right behind ya."

We head down stairs and everyone starts clapping as if we had just arrived from Alabama, not leaving for Alabama.

The Disturbed

None the less it felt great to feel so much love from all of our friends and family. I walk up to Mom and whisper in her ear, "Thank you, Mom." She gives me a big smile and says.
"You're welcome Derek. I love you, and I'm sure going to miss you son. Go try the dip and shish-kabobs, they are amazing."

She says with a wink. Boy was she right about the kabobs; they are nothing short of amazing. The whole party is amazing and to see all my former classmates again was awesome. Mom always made home feel like home, which also brought back the struggle inside myself I've had about leaving, but at the same time, I know it's time to go find my own life, go down my own road so to speak.

I was mingling with a few of my old friends, enjoying some good food, and trying to soak in the moments I have left in Cali.

My drink was getting low so I decided to get a refill. Just as I look up from the crowd, I see him in between the cars parked near the patio off our side yard. He stares at me a long time then again gives me that smirk. This time I am pissed. This is my house, my fuckin party and the hell if this guy is going to keep fucking with my life. I rush outside after him. As I rush out the door, the screen slamming behind me, I turn the corner but I don't see him. I start looking in between the cars and around the house, finding nothing. Then I look back at the house, I see Mom looking at me as Jazz comes running out to meet her.

"Derek? Are you alright son? You ran out of the house so fast I got worried."

Dad comes out of the house and stands next to Mom too waiting for me to answer her. I'm lost for words. I mean, if I tell them the truth I will surely feel like I am letting them down. I just can't.

"I saw a dog, a beautiful dog out here, looked like a puppy but I can't find it now. Sure was cute and I didn't want it getting hit by a car."

"Well good grief, you scared the beans out of me. I must have the mommy jitters, I guess?"

The whole time I am talking about this imaginary dog I am looking around for this guy, this thing, but again he, it, is nowhere to be found. I try and rid myself of my pissed off expression on my face because that would not make any sense while I am out here looking for a puppy. Then Dad asked,

"Derek, you sure you're alright son, you have been on edge for days now?" Knowing he can see through my expression change, which I almost thought I got away with.

"Yeah, yeah Dad, I'm good really. I gaze over the area again, then head in the house to get my drink.

"You know I just may get a dog after I get settled in Alabama. I think that may just help me adjust to all the changes too.

The Disturbed

"I say as I pass by Mom and Dad to get that drink.
"Well Derek, just make sure you get settled first."
"Copy that Dad!"
I smile and walk inside. Jazz follows me inside.
"What's going on with you Derek? You're not having those delusions again are you?"
"Nah man. I'm good really, no worries."
"Alright, just checking on my best friend."
"Sure, sure, thanks Jazz. You're a great friend man".
I say to him as I pat him on the shoulder.
"Let's get back to the party huh?"

"Hey all, let's get to the gifts…Derek, honey come over here…you too Jazz, time to open some going away gifts."

We opened the gifts which was so much fun. Mom and Dad gave me things like a gas-can, portable heater, sleeping bags that are insulated for Jazz and I, some dishes for our new place, flashlights, batteries, and an envelope with money which I was so very grateful for. It was all really great. Some of our friends got us blankets, and cups, stuff that dudes use like shaving cream as a joke. We all had a great laugh about that. Dad got me a really nice pocket-knife, which I will cherish forever, it sure reminded me of our fishing trip we just had.

It gets late as friends start to say their personal good byes. Each one so touching making me wish I was not leaving this amazing place. But I am grateful for all of them and all the memories we all have. We say good-bye to the last of the guests and I help Mom clean up a bit before heading to my room. Jazz comes up for a few minutes and we make plans to meet to get lunch tomorrow and start packing our things up.

"Hey Derek, great party, it was great seeing everyone again, going to miss it here."

"Yeah, me too man. I have been thinking about that for days but we have to grow up sometime huh."

"Yeah, you're right. So, tomorrow about noon for lunch and then we'll get packing, right?"

"Yep, time to get packed man. Kind of exciting when you think about it."

"You're right Derek, we just need to get over being homesick then we will be fine." Jazz laughs as he starts down the stairs.

"See ya tomorrow man."

"Yeah."

"Late."

I get cozy in my room, take my meds, and I am off to bed. What an amazing day, I think to myself, besides my damn delusions again. Probably the anxiety from knowing I am moving. I'm sure all will be fine once we get going.

CHAPTER 4

Need for Change

The time had come for Jazz and me to set out for Alabama. I was not looking forward to the long hours of driving, but I sure was looking forward to the adventure of it all. Jazz and I finished packing the trailer and sat for a few minutes with Mom and Dad before it was to time to get going.

"Derek, you got everything you need son?" Mom asked worriedly.

"Yes, Mom I think we are set for our adventure." Dad looked a bit nervous, probably because he knew what long road-trips were like.

"You boys call if you have any trouble along the way, anytime now, okay?"

Wow, I had never seen Dad so worried in my life. But, I guess we were all feeling a bit of separation anxiety, and the thought of a four to five-day trip was a bit unsettling for sure.

"Will do Dad. We'll be fine."

I said, as I tried to reassure Dad and Mom, we would have a safe trip. Well, I decided it was time to go before my parents made me stay or made me more nervous about leaving. Jazz seemed fine to be going except for missing his little sister who looked up to him in everything. Jazz had said good bye to his family an hour prior to us getting ready to leave from my house.

"I'll call you every day until we get there and even after until we get settled. How's that?"

"Sounds great son"

I give Mom a big hug and a kiss on the cheek.

"I love you Derek."

"I love you too Mom." I go to shake Dad's hand and he pulls me in for a hug.

"Come here you! I am going to miss you son. Be sure and call, no forgetting and making your mother worry, ya hear?"

"Sure, thing Dad."

Jazz and I get in the car. I see tears in Mom's eyes again which makes my soul ache. Dad on the other hand is trying not to show his emotions, although I sense them, as manly as he is.

"Okay call you guys later, love you."

"We will be waiting for your call Derek"

If I know my Mom, she will be glued to the chair next to the phone all night.

We all wave as I step on the gas to leave. Stomachs in knots as I drive away from the only security I have ever known.

"We will be fine."

I tell Jazz, almost to reassure myself.

"Yep! No worries there bud, we got this."

Jazz puts on some music as we start on the freeway.

We drive all day and night stopping only for restroom breaks and gas. Jazz decides to drive for a while, so I can phone Mom.

"Hey Mom, just wanted to call and let you know we are doing fine. We are going to drive through the night taking turns and probably get a room tomorrow evening to get some good rest before we keep going. We are almost through Arizona now."

"Wow, that's great to hear son, glad you guys are doing fine. Lord knows I will sleep better now."

"I know Mom; I figured you would be waiting by the phone. Mom, can you let Dad know we are great too and I love you guys so much. I will call again tomorrow okay."

"Okay son, we will talk to you tomorrow then. Drive safe"

"Will do Mom, goodnight"
"Goodnight son"
We hang up the phone and I lay my head against the headrest. Man, am I beat from driving for hours.
"Jazz you got this for an hour or two?"
"Yep, got it bro, catch a nap man. I will wake you when we get close to needing gas again, how's that?"
"Sounds good, thanks man."
A couple of hours pass by and I feel a nudge.
"Hey Derek, we are at the gas station now."
"Oh damn, how long I been out man?"
"About three hours or so. It's about four a.m. man."
"Okay, hey I'll get the gas."
"Alright man, I'm going to hit the can while you are doing that. I've got to piss like a race horse."

Jazz laughs as he heads to the gas station bathroom.
I am pumping gas and start to stare off into space. Gazing around the area I see that fucker again. That faceless fuck who keeps taunting me. I shake my head, thinking to myself I am just still maybe dazed from my nap. But I look again, and he is standing right beside the gas station building. He looks at me again, turns and is gone.
'What the fuck?' I say to myself. Just then Jazz comes out of the building. I finish pumping the gas and put the cap on.

The Disturbed

"Derek, what's wrong man you look like you saw a ghost or something? You good man?"
"Yeah man, I'm good. The bathroom free?"
"As far as I know."
"Alright be right back."
I slip into the bathroom and wash my face off with water hoping it might wake me up. Finish my business and walk back to the car.
"You good man?"
"Yep, let's roll."
I take the wheel while Jazz puts some music on and then passes out. I drive for a few more hours as I watch the sun come up I can't stop thinking about seeing that faceless fuck again. I really need to get a different medication because these are sure in the hell not working. Sure, feels like he's following me though. One of the first things I'm doing when I get to Alabama besides finding a place is finding a therapist for sure.

Jazz wakes up and takes over the driving again. We switch off all day until evening when we decide to get a motel for the night, shower and get some solid sleep. We've been on the road two days now and it's time for a break. Some warm food wouldn't hurt either. Man, I'm missing Mom's cooking about now. We get a room. Jazz picks a bed and crashes. I turn on the TV for some noise and hop in the shower to wash off the two-day grub. I'm in the shower and I hear the door open.

"Hello, Jazz?"

I peak out of the shower curtain and the door is cracked open. Feeling nervous I shut off the water, grab a towel and step out to take a look.

Jazz is sound asleep on the bed he crashed on. What the fuck? Is this place haunted too. I didn't see that faceless fuck again but who the hell opened the door? The motel door is locked.

I dry my hair with the towel and get into bed. Almost too tired to care I start watching a show that's on the TV and pass out cold.

Morning comes, and they have a Café next to the motel. I wait for Jazz to get cleaned up, and I watch the news for a while to catch up on events of the past couple of days.

Jazz and I head over to the café where they are serving biscuits and gravy.

"See Jazz, this is the best part of our adventure, good food along the way."

"You got that right Derek. I'm so ready for some hot bacon and eggs right now man."

The waitress brings our breakfast to the table and we grub like there's no tomorrow. Although this café food is great it's nothing like Mom's, that's for sure. We finish up our coffee and Jazz gets the bill while I take care of the tip and it's time to hit the road. We check out of our room and I start off driving again. Within a few hours we reach Wellington, Alabama our destination. It had been a long trip, but we made it a bit longer by stopping to get some good food and rest along the way. What's a road trip without a little pleasure? We roll into the city and spot a car on the side of the road. It's a girl who is having car trouble.

"Hey Jazz, that girl is all alone with car issues, we've got to help man."
"Alright, let's check it out see if she needs anything."

We roll up to her, I get out of the car, and walk over to her.
"Hello, I'm Derek, that's my friend Jazz, we just got here from California and noticed you are having some trouble with your car. Wanted to know if there is anything we can do to help?

"Hello Derek, that is mighty kind of you, my name is Lacy. It's very nice to meet you."
She says as she extends her hand to shake mine.
"Actually, I need some gas; I seem to have run out. I think the gage is not working anymore or something. I was trying to get to school and it just died."
"Well, I can sure help with that. Would you like to come with us to get the gas? Or you can wait here, it is up to you."

"Sure, I will come along, you seem like a very sweet city boy and I appreciate the help."
"Great! Well, hop in and let's get you some gas."

We head down the road about three miles or so and fill up my gas can for her. That was one of Mom's going away gifts, never knew it would come in handy like this but, all things happen for a reason that is for sure.

Heading back to her car we start more small talk and I realize she goes to the very college I'm transferring to and for some reason I feel an excitement well up within me. She seems to stare at me, but I don't mind one bit, she is just beautiful and sweet as my Mom's apple pie.

"Okay, she's all filled-up; at least until you get to a gas station to really fill-up. Lacy, it's been great meeting you and talking with you this whole time, sure hope to see you in school."

"Same here Derek, hey would you like to exchange numbers so we can keep in touch?"

"Sure, that sounds perfect!"

"Great! Here's my number, text me, and I will add you to my phone okay."

"Sounds good Lacy, thanks."

"No! Thank you guys for stopping and caring, I truly appreciate it. See you in school Derek, and hope to talk to you when you get a chance as well. Take care and good luck getting settled."

The Disturbed

"Thanks." She says as she waves driving off in the direction of the college.

Jazz starts in on me.

"Dude what was all that? I didn't know you were going to get a number I thought we were just going to help out or something."

"Hey, don't get your panties in a wad dude, I was helping out, she also seems like a great girl. What are you jealous?"

"Nah, I'm not jealous, just happened pretty fast is all. We just got here man."

"Well I think it's great. Now I have someone to help me out around here, at least at school. Hey, she seems like a nice girl and I can't wait to get to know her."

"Well, more power to ya than bro, just be careful. I mean you just got out of a bad, serious relationship so maybe go easy huh."

"Chill Jazz, I'm in no hurry man relax!"

"Yeah, I guess dude. Do your thing." About an about into town I stated to call on houses available for rent in the area. I was in the mood to go look at some.

"Hey, let's go find this place we're supposed to rent huh. Come'on man moving here is supposed to be a good thing why not start now when we roll into the city, works for me man."

"I'm with you on that bro."

Just then the phone rings, I answer it and it's the landlord of one of the houses I was really interested in seeing.

53

"Hello?"

"Hello there, may I speak to Derek please? This is Mr. Ross; I own the house for rent on Tom Reeds Rd. I need to know if he is interested in renting here or not because I have to get this place out, you know?"

"Yes, hello Mr. Ross I was about to call you. Yes, we are very interested and would like very much to come see it now if at all possible. We just arrived in Alabama this morning actually."

"That would be fine; you can come now if you'd like."

"Great! We are on our way there now sir, thank you for calling. See you soon."

"Alright then, see you soon."

What perfect timing, everything seemed to just be lining up just right as soon as we arrived in Alabama. We found the address and took a look at the house. It was perfect, and thank God, it was ready to move in to. We signed the lease then started to unpack the car and trailer we had rented for our stuff. It's weird to finally have my own place although it is Jazz's place too. It's like I'm truly on my own now and it felt really good. I was a bit nervous about Mr. Ross stating that he had had a hard time renting the house due to the fact it was a very isolated area. I had heard that many referred to this area of Alabama as a "hillbilly hell" due to the fact so many unexplained deaths occurred in the past two years. That part didn't sit too well with me knowing I had just moved here to be less stressed. Sure rather be here than back in the city though. That was getting to me and the stress seemed to really take its toll. My parents' house was in a nice part of the mountains in Big Bear, but I still had a long commute every day to the city which seemed to stay with me anyway when I got back to the beautiful mountains. So, I was glad to finally be home, in 'my home.' Man did that sound good, and it felt good to say, free is more like it.

My next plan was to take back the trailer in the morning, find out where Alabama State University was, and get registered for my classes. My plans were to later get a full-time job working on a farm or two while I got my Master's degree, but I was willing to take anything for work until I got familiar with this place. At least I was willing to get my hands dirty at some job to do what needed to be done to pay the bills and have a nice life here. The house rent was pretty low; much lower than California, that about shocked the hell out of me. Come to think of it, it was time to call Mom, and give her the update on our grand adventure.

"Hey Mom, how's everything with you and Dad? We just got here and already have the house so things are amazing so far."

"Oh Derek, that is great to hear son, I am so very proud of you. So, you all moved in?"

"Yeah, we moved everything in just a few hours ago. You would like it here Mom, it's kind of like Big Bear with all the wooded trees everywhere. So that part makes me feel close to home. Miss, you and Dad though."

"Well Derek, sounds like you and Jazz are finding your way just fine. I have no worries you will do great in college and be happy there son. Just stay focused and remember your goals okay?"

"Yes Mom, I will. I will call again in a few days okay? I have to get my classes and find a local job to keep us going here, and Jazz plans on doing the same. I don't have to keep mooching off you and Dad. But I sure do appreciate both of you so very much and your support means the world to me Mom."

"I know you do Derek, that's what we are here for son. I miss you dearly and pray for you every day, keep doing great things son, and we will talk with you soon."

"Will do Mom, hey thanks again, I miss you too. Talk soon."

I hung the phone up feeling a bit home-sick, but as I looked around that all passed pretty quickly. I mean, it's fucking beautiful here and what's not to love about this place. I haven't seen the fucker that follows me since the motel, but I never really saw him there thank God.

The Disturbed

I know that door did not open by itself, and that for me was enough. Being at this house kind of felt like being back at the cabin where Dad and I last went fishing. It has the same type of surroundings anyway and if Jazz was not here I would probably feel a lot more freaked out about being in the woods. The house has two bedrooms and one bathroom. I chose the bedroom in the back side of the house with the sliding glass doors. I thought that it would be cool to look at the moon or sky from my bed at night. There was a view of the back woods from my bedroom and although that was a bit eerie it also gave me a bit of peace being with nature and all. Maybe it's because I am gone from the stressful city, on my own, in my own peaceful place. I'm not sure but I'm sure hoping it lasts.

Time to get some dinner, settle in for the night at the new house. I am hoping I sleep well, but I have my meds to help with that too. Got to get ready for tomorrow and map out all the places I have to get to, seeing that I am new here it's not like I can just put my brain on autopilot and drive straight there like before, at least not yet. I was thinking about calling that nice girl Lacy to maybe meet for coffee, but maybe I should give it one more day. Like Jazz said I shouldn't go rushing things, we did just get here, but I am sure it's all the excitement in the air from the whole adventure. As for Jazz, he's already crashed out on the floor over in the corner, but hell who could blame him it's been a rough three days for both of us.

We already picked our rooms, so I go in mine and start to unpack my things. We haven't got any furniture yet, so we will definitely have to man this place up a bit. The house came with a stove and a small fridge which helps a lot at this point of our journey. Still feels like camping though, and something I will have to get used to. I yell to Jazz that I am going to run to the corner store and get some bread and stuff and ask if he want to go with.

"Hey Jazz, dude I am going to get some bread and stuff at the corner store do you want to go with man?"

"Nah, I'm cool right here man, see ya when you get back."

"Cool!"

I take off as the sun starts to set to locate the corner store I know we passed on the way here. The roads are eerie with no people around, but that is to be expected here in the country anyway. As I keep driving I start to feel as if I wish Jazz would have come along, but I am a grown ass man, I got this. It's dark as hell out here and no lights but the headlights of the car. I left the trailer-hitch on the car being too tired to take it off, and knowing I would only have to put it back on in the morning. I make a right on the main road and keep driving realizing this is a bit more then I was expecting. There were no lights for miles, so I was creeped out for sure. I tried not to think about it and just kept driving knowing there would be a store down

The Disturbed

the road as long as I kept going. I turned the music up a bit to take my mind off of being alone and keep my brain from wondering. Finally, I see a gas station about five miles down and the small corner store right next door which was almost about to close. I got here just in time. Rushing inside the store I grab up some bread, lunch meat, mayo, and some mustard, chips, soda, and I am out of there. On the way out, I see a sign on the cashier window that says 'help wanted' and decide to see if I could get an application. I walk up to the window of the cashier.

"Excuse me sir? Are you still hiring here for a cashier?"
"Yes, we are still hiring. You interested?"
"Yes sir, sure am. May I have an application please?"
"Sure, you new to these parts? You don't sound like you are from around here?"
"Well, actually I just moved here to go to college. I live right down the street off of Tom Reeds Rd."
"Oh, I see, did you just move into the house with the red bricks?"
"Yes, why has it been for rent for a while?"
"Well, there was a family murdered about six months ago who lived in that house. They didn't find their bodies inside the house just in the back-forest area. Kind of creepy to me."
"Yes, wow, I was not told about that at all and we moved in today."

"Well, stay safe over there. I guess they caught the guy so not too much to fear anymore. Hope that doesn't ruin your view of the area, we got some great people around here."

"No, it doesn't but I sure appreciate you telling me and I will have this application back to you in the morning."

"Sounds good, I won't be here but you can leave it here and I will take a look at it tomorrow afternoon."

"Thank you, I didn't get your name. I'm Derek."

"Sam, nice to meet you Derek, I'll be giving you a call either way okay"

"Thanks again Sam."

Rushing to my car I toss everything across the seat and sit there for a moment in shock. All of a sudden, my home felt a lot less cozy that's for sure. It was certainly something I was not going to tell Mom, even though they had caught the guy. I was wondering if I should tell Jazz, probably being that he lives there with me. I start the car and think about what Sam had just told me all the way back to the house. For some strange reason, I wanted to know more about the story, more about the family. I felt if I did it would help me put some rest to my living here now. After all, I was now on a lease for a year, and all of a sudden it seemed like it was going to be a long year.

The Disturbed

Morning came and it was time to return the trailer and get started on my day. I tossed and turned all night as I thought about what had happened to the people who lived here prior to me and Jazz. Although I didn't know the details I sure needed to. When Jazz woke up I told him and to my surprise he was not too alarmed about it at all. I mean it shook him up a bit but he was not tripping-out like I was about now having to live here after finding out. I hoped that after I did the research on the murders I would find rest in that and hopefully be able to sleep better. I finished filling out the application for the corner gas-station that I picked up last night. I felt pretty good about the possibilities of working there after meeting Sam, the owner of the place. Then I decided to go get my classes. So, I collected my college transcripts I needed to register, my computer, and I was off to find my way around a new city, and new state.

Jazz and I set out for the day. I drop off the application first then I was off to drop off the trailer. We pull in and I see a familiar face that I have seen back in California. I walk over to take a closer look and realize its John Stevens from my last college.

"Hey Jazz, look it's John! Do you remember John Stevens from school man? He was the college quarterback."

"Yeah, I remember that asshole."

"He wasn't always an asshole man. We had some fun times."

"Yeah, when he was not trying to prove he was better than everyone else, even at the game."

"You're right on that aspect I guess."

"Hey John, how you been man? It's me Derek from college back in Cali."

"Hey Derek. What's up man? How the hell are you?"

"Life is sweet man, just got here from Cali, from the looks of it you just got here too huh?"

"Yeah man, I just moved here to live with my Mom. Got tired of the city."

"Jazz and I came here for the same reason. You remember Jazz, right?"

"Yeah, hey how's it going Jazz, been a long-time man."

"Yep, it's been about a year or so. I hadn't seen you around college much before we graduated anyway."

"I had to drop out to take care of my Mom after my Dad died. So, I decided to move here to finish up my classes, and stay close to Mom. It's a lot slower paced here than in Cali ya know. You guys will have to get used to that."

"Yah, we plan to start back in college here too. Glad to see you again. Maybe we can hang-out sometime and throw-back a few beers or something?"

The Disturbed

"Sure, let me get your number, and let's make some plans."

"Sounds good man, hey, we'll talk later."

We exchange numbers and I go inside to do the paperwork to return the trailer. The guy goes outside checks for dents and comes back in, I pay what's owed, and we are on our way. We head off to the college as the GPS leads and I think to give Lacy a call to see what she's up to and find out if she's on campus or not. I dial the number and it rings, but went to voicemail.

"Hello Lacy, its Derek from the other day....the gas man hahaha.

Sorry, I am not good with messages, but I wanted to say hello and see if maybe you wanted to meet-up? I am at the college now getting ready to register. Anyway, give me a call when you get this if you like, (555)748-1711. Thanks.

"Damn!" I hate leaving voicemails, I feel like I sound like an ass every time and I get so tongue-tied. I was hoping to talk to her, but at least I got to hear her voice. I park the car and grab my paperwork.

"Jazz you coming with?"

"Nah, I have been thinking I will hold off for a semester until I get used to being here and more comfortable, or at least find a job."

"Alright man, sounds like a plan. Getting a job first sounds like a great idea anyway to help us out. That's why I am already looking myself. One application in this morning. Oh yeah!"

I leave Jazz in the car to chill and go hunting for the registers office. It wasn't too hard to find seeing that I found a wall map of the school. I walk in and am greeted by the clerk.
"Can I help you?"
"Hello, my name is Derek, I just moved here from California and would like to transfer my college credits here and register for classes for the Fall please. I hope I am not too late."
"Nope you're not too late, our college rarely gets all its classes full, probably because it is in the country where the population of people is a bit lower than California. Do you know what classes you desire to take? And do you have your transcripts?"
"Sure do, and yes, I would like to take Criminal Justice, which I also obtained my bachelors in, I brought all that information with me."
"Great! Let's get you enrolled."

Just then I look up and see Lacy walking down the hall in the registers office. I know I just met her, but for some reason my heart started to beat really fast. I was not sure if it was because I was worried about what she thought about my message or the fact that she is so damn beautiful. Whatever the case I sure liked the feeling. She notices me. Our eyes meet, she smiles big, and walks toward me. She leans in and whispers...

"Hi Derek, got your message, call you later okay. You trying to hook-up with the girl whose car you fixed?" She says with a cute smirk.

"I will be waiting for it." I reply back.

Oh my gosh, was that too much? I thought to myself, but she obviously seemed interested, so chill Derek. Man did she smell good, I mean so good, and that voice. I think I'm in love.

I got done getting all my Fall classes then asked if I could use the library computers for a while. I know Jazz is in the car waiting, but I have to do some research on those murders so I can sleep. I send him a quick text to let him know I will be a while longer. I am worried what I will find out as well, but that doesn't stop me from wanting to know, that's for sure. I have to know more. I am directed in the area of the library and find it fairly quickly. I sit down and type in my street address for starters and a bunch of articles come up, I start to read. My mouth drops open as I take-in the details of the findings, and the evidence that was recovered. The information was so detailed I felt chills knowing I lived so very close to all of this and where it had happened. I felt connected in a weird way to something that was already in the past, recent past, but still too close to home. The article had said the guy had been caught, but what he did to them was turning my stomach as I read. They had not only been killed brutally, but they were cut up in pieces and buried in shallow graves almost as if the guy wanted to be caught. That's the sense I got about it anyway. To top it off, there was no motive for the murders other than the guy worked temporarily for the husband of the family. He had been let go for not showing up to work. The articles also said he had allegedly been caught stealing supplies from the company before he was fired. Senseless killings. I tried to wrap my head around what I was reading so I could somehow give myself some closure in some type of way to be at peace with what had happened. How was I going to cope with living there a year without it feeling like home? Jazz seemed to be doing alright with it so far which made me wonder if he truly understood what had taken place. I mean how could he just nonchalantly say, "Oh wow?"

I read as much as my stomach could take, and wondered if it was wise that I had done that, but at the same time I needed to know. I did feel like I got some kind of closure at least in being able to grieve the names and the sadness even though it really didn't belong to me, it was more out of respect that I wanted to know. I went

The Disturbed

home and went to the back of the house alone although I was freaked out. I wanted to say a prayer and say I was sorry for what had happened to them. I had to share what was on my heart letting them know the guys had been caught even though many before me probably had, it was something I had to do. I had asked Jazz if he wanted to go out to say a prayer with me but he said I was tripping and to just let it go. I sure felt better after I went outside and prayed, although I didn't know if they knew I prayed, but I knew I cared, and felt better inside for doing so.

The phone rang, it was beautiful Lacy. We talked for about an hour which was nice because I got to know a lot more about her. I didn't want to tell her anything about where I lived other than I loved having moved to Alabama. I thought for sure it would freak her out. We had one class together starting in the Fall. I was excited, but also wondered if I would be able to stay focused in that class, after all she was already pretty distracting. Earlier in the day I had made an appointment with my new therapist here. It was time to get to sleep, time to let all that had happened in the day go, time to start my new life here in Alabama. I felt prayer helped and they approved as well for some strange reason. Tomorrow it was time to go meet my knew therapist Dr. Susan Wright, now there was a place I could probably get some help with my feelings about where I lived at least. I mean I felt I had some closure, but to talk about it, I thought, was a good idea for sure. I took my meds and off to sleep I went.

Mom called the other day, and I had a chance to tell her about Lacy. I was a bit excited on the phone. I guess she could hear it in my voice because she asked if I was in love with her.

Nervously, I said

"Yes, I am Mom" and waited for her reply, which was quite nice.

"I'm very happy for you Derek, and hope she is the one." Of course, I hoped the same as well. I also gave her an update on school.

"It's nice to know Lacy is in the same college as you son, and have the same goals." Mom said.

"So, how is work going?" We had the normal chit chat that goes on with family long distance, which was nice because I was about to change my schedule and find a better paying job. I told her I would have something new to share with her next time I called, which she said she couldn't wait to hear. Mom missed me; I could hear it in her voice. I asked about Dad and she said he was busy as usual, but he had been asking her if she had heard from me lately. It was good to hear they were doing well, and as always hanging-up the phone from our

The Disturbed

conversation made me miss home again. That was probably one of the reasons why I did not call as much as I should. I looked forward to the coming months, and the good news I would share with them as my life took on yet more changes. I sure hoped the both of them could come visit sometime or maybe Lacy and I could go out there. I sure wanted them to meet her, she was the one.

CHAPTER 5

Finding True Love

My classes start in about a week. Sam called me yesterday about the gas-station job, and told me I could start next week. Within a week I was working at a gas station a couple of miles from my newly rented apartment. The job wasn't what I was looking for at the moment, but I took it until I was able to start my classes, and find a couple of farmers looking for some good help in the area. Lacy and I had been talking on the phone every night for the past week. If I wasn't working I was talking to her. Jazz was looking for work, but he was having a bit more trouble than me because I had the car all the time. He asked if he could use the car for a couple of nights just to put in some applications and get out of the house, I agreed. I mean we were out in the country now it's not like he could just walk to the city. I went to my therapist appointment a few days ago with Dr. Susan Wright and was able to talk about where I live, the move, and give her the medical files obtained by my last therapist from California. I also decided to stay on the medication for a couple of more weeks anyway, due to the fact I had not had any more delusions since the drive here. I was feeling pretty settled and pretty excited about Lacy and I even though it was very new. I sure was trying not to rush our closeness but I had to admit it was a challenge. Classes started two weeks ago, and I was hoping that Jazz could find a job soon so he could find a route to work, and back so I would have the car for work and school.

I had school papers to start on when I got home, and was not looking forward to having to have to walk home by any means. It was getting late. I had called Jazz to see if he could pick me up from work, and there was not reply on his cell. I was getting off work in about twenty minutes and it was a five mile walk home, which I was not looking forward to, in the case that he didn't respond, but I had to get home. Getting ready to close the gas station down, Jazz never returned my call, so I decided I could use the exercise anyway trying to keep

The Disturbed

a positive attitude about it all, it was not like I had a choice at this point to do anything else. He was sure going to hear it from me though when I did get home or he got home which ever came first. I mean, I thought it was pretty nice of me to lend him the car, and this was pretty disrespectful to say the least.

It was at the dusk when I started off walking. The fog was rolling in just as thick as the night before, but I those nights was able to drive home. Tonight I could hear the light howling of the wind, the owls, and the crickets chirping. As I started walking from the gas station on the corner of Chaser and Yearn I was a bit nervous to say the least. I felt uneasy as I thought about that faceless fuck, how he had followed me so many times before and what had happened behind the house where I lived didn't help my thoughts. I had an eerie feeling; I felt I was being followed again. Not followed by anyone in the open, but by someone or something that seemed to be hiding. This night seemed quieter than normal except for the sound of the wind, the owls, and crickets hidden in the tall oak trees surrounding the streets I took to get to work and home. This night as I took the same route home I saw a white form inside the bushes, the same white form I had seen so many times before. I could not quite make out what it was, but it looks like that faceless fuck again. He was tall and seemed to want to get my attention, but didn't want to be known. I started to walk faster, humming to myself the last song I had heard on the radio before I left work. It wasn't helping much. Then I started to think about Lacy, and that was the only thing that seemed to help, and provide a slight distraction. There were no cars, no headlights in the distance, no other houses, just trees for miles. The further I got down the street the more alone I felt, and the more fear set in my mind, which seemed to overwhelm me as thoughts raced through my mind.

God, why did I lend him my car? I thought to myself. Why after all of my hard work and commitment was I walking home scared? I had overcome so much and to be in this place was not foreseen, had it been I would have said a big, "No" to Jazz. But, like with everything we face in life if we only knew then what we know now, that's just not realistic way to live or think. I realize I am babbling to myself to try and pass time. The feeling of being followed was getting stronger and I wanted to run. My walk turned into a quick-paced run as my insides shook with fear. I was now about a mile and a half away from home, but it seemed like I just left and had five miles still to go. As my pace picked up, I could hear the rustling of leaves in the bushes on the side of the dirt road. I wondered if it was him. Was it him or a damn animal? I thought to myself was I freaking my own self out. Was I giving myself a panic attack? I wanted to be at home all of a sudden, I mean home with Mom and Dad. I reverted to needing them and feeling like I could not make it on my own. It was late, and I didn't want to call home. If I called Lacy she would probably hear the fear in my voice. There was no getting out of this and no help in sight. It was time to grow up and deal with how I was feeling all alone. No one to bail me out, not that I had had that before, but having Mom and Dad around sure felt more secure, and that was sure what I wanted to feel now. I was a grown ass man, but inside I felt like a scared little boy hoping to make it home in one piece. Finally, I could see my house, then saw my car. I could feel my face turn red with anger now.

I had finally gotten home that evening. Jazz was asleep on the couch we had just bought, with a movie running on the play screen over, and over. I walk up to him.

"What the hell Jazz? Why couldn't you answer the phone or at least come give me the car man?" I was pissed, so pissed I could feel my ears burning with heat.

"Sorry man, I fell asleep and I didn't hear my phone man. What! Where is my phone?"

"Jazz you are so irresponsible and it's getting on my fucking nerves man. I mean you have had a few days with my car, and I feel that you aren't doing shit with your life man!"

"I put in one application today man, I guess I am a bit depressed. I mean life seems to be going great for you, and I am struggling at everything I do."

"Yeah, but at least you have someone here who cares enough to help you man, but you have to want to make shit better for yourself Jazz. I hate to sound like a dick, but you can't use the car anymore dude, I mean shit I had to walk for five miles after working 7 hours, and I still have a paper for class I have to finish. You just don't seem to get it. I know we haven't been here long, but if you want shit to change bad enough you can make shit happen dude."

"Yeah, I hear you Derek, sorry for being a douche man and making you have to walk, that's pretty fucked up of me. Sorry dude I truly am. Glad you made it home safe man."

"Yeah, me too, it's okay. I will try and help you as much as I can with transportation, but please step up to the plate here Jazz, alright? Like I said I am not trying to be a dick, but I can't do everything here by myself you know."

"Yeah, man I got it."

"Alright man, I'm off to get some writing done. Late."

"Late man. Hey, take me to town with ya tomorrow so I can look around for hiring signs, okay man?"

"Okay man, not a problem."

The Disturbed

I retreat to my room, and boy did it feel good to finally get home. I couldn't get that sighting of that damn guy out of my mind again. This scared me more than all of the other times because I was not only alone in a new state, but I didn't have my car either. It haunted me so much so that I had a nightmare that evening. Finding Jazz asleep really pissed me off. Ever since we have gotten here he has been a real asshole. I mean I am trying to help him get a job or something, hoping he would just get motivated, but instead he's done the opposite. I don't even know if he had even gone to put in applications or lazed around all day somewhere. He was always jealous of my new-found love and it was really pissing me off. Now, that he didn't even have the consideration to call or pick me up from work with me pulling all this weight of classes and a job.

I didn't talk much about what happened on the way home, not even to Jazz because I wanted to put the past behind me so to speak, and start over. I seemed to do that a lot, start over I mean, hoping for a different outcome. I also didn't want anyone who didn't know anything about my past to get the wrong impression about me, especially my new girlfriend. I sure didn't want to appear crazy to her. I had put in a few extra hours of studying to try and keep up with the demands of homework, and the night shift at my new job. I wondered if I had over-reacted a little about him not picking me up, but I vowed to never lend my car to Jazz again, and I told him I wouldn't. I felt it was a bit harsh, but after all I had been through I was done with the games. I was not walking home from the gas station again, that's for sure. It was time for Jazz to grow-up a bit and take on some of this responsibility.

I talked to Lacy about my issues with Jazz and she agreed with me. I hated talking about my best-friend I had grown-up with to someone else, but at the same time I needed some type of outlet. I trusted Lacy from the very beginning. She was amazing, and she trusted me the same. Although we had not known each other for very long it seemed like we had known each other for years.

Morning came and to my surprise Jazz was up and waiting for me on the couch. I had classes today, and was going to go to lunch with Lacy. I was also hoping that Jazz had some luck with finding a job as well. I walked in and told Jazz I was ready to go, we grabbed our stuff, and headed out. I decided to get something to eat on the way to school, hopefully with Lacy. I dropped Jazz off at the shopping center coffee shop and pulled over to give Lacy a call to see if she wanted to meet for a bite to eat. She answered:

"Hello?"
   "Hello, hey Lacy, it's me."
   "Hey Derek, you heading to class?"

"Yah, but I wanted to know if you ate, or if you would like to get some coffee or something in the cafeteria with me before class?"
"Oh yeah, sure that sounds great, can't wait."
"Nice, I will be there in about ten minutes, okay."
"Great! See you soon."

I started to drive like a bat out of hell to get to her which made me realize I was truly digging on this girl. I mean, I could fall in love with her and fast. I felt I already was, which scared me a bit but, at the same time excited the hell out of me, and there was no stopping it. I get to the cafeteria where I see beautiful Lacy waiting for me just outside the door. I walk up to her, and greet her with a kiss on the lips. I feel a rush of desire shoot through my body. I was captivated and thought this is the one. We had not slept together although we had gotten pretty close while cuddling, and the desire for each other was extreme. We knew it would happen soon but we weren't rushing either. We were silently waiting for the right moment. I think she felt the rush of desire flow through her as well and for a second we both were thinking to ditch class today as we looked at each other deep in the eyes. I pulled myself together, grabbed her hand and took her into the cafeteria for some quick breakfast.

"So, what are you doing after class today?"

"Depends what you are doing." She says with a big beautiful smile.

"I was wondering since I don't have to work tonight if you would like to come share some Chinese, and a movie together?"

"I would love to. Sounds wonderful babe." She called me babe...I turn red in the face as I feel the heat in my cheeks.

"Nice! Sounds amazing to me too, I can't wait." And oh, how I meant that, I was so going to be distracted during class. It was nice to have a night off from work too after that long walk. Lacy had a way of making me feel so much more comfortable at home than when she was not there. I guess with her with me I didn't feel alone. She had a way of making me feel at ease even having the knowledge of what had happened there at the house. It was clear I was falling and falling hard. It sure seemed she was as well and I wanted to be alone with her.

We got done with our breakfast went too our two classes one of which we had together. I walked her to our first class and sat next to her. We paid attention as much as possible while we passed notes back and forth. We could have texted but we didn't want to give away the fact that we were doing something other than paying attention to the instructor. I felt like I was in high school all over again and I loved it. Class came to an end, and we went to grab lunch, then it was back to our last class of the day. After lunch, I walked her to her classes, kissed her on the lips again feeling that rush of desire fill my body. We had been seeing each other for almost three weeks, and talking for four weeks so I could feel the desire was mutual. Just than my phone rang:

"Hello?"
"Hey Derek, its Jazz man. Guess what? I got an interview tomorrow. I wanted to know if you could possibly take me man. It's at eleven a.m."
"Nice! Jazz, sure I can take you on the way to school. No problem man. Hey! And good job dude, proud of you man." I didn't want to sound like his mother, but I felt bad for being an ass last night, and I was proud of him.

"Oh hey, just an FYI man, Lacy is coming over tonight for some dinner and a movie."
"Cool, you can pick me up on the way back home, tonight right?"
"Sure, not a problem man...see you at the same spot in about three hours okay. I have one more class."
"No problem, I will find something to do. See you in a bit man, late"
"Late bro."

After walking Lacy to her next class, my walk had turned into a jog to make it to my next class on time. The only thing on my mind that I can't shake is being with her alone tonight, holding her close while we watch a movie. I start to day dream in class wondering if Lacy is doing the same thing. I smile to myself then look up, and notice the instructor is looking straight at me. I slowly scoot up, sitting up-right in my chair. Time to focus, at least try to. Three hours later, and class finally is out. It's funny how when you are waiting or wanting something, time seems to just drag on. I walk fast to meet Lacy at her class, she sees me, and walks faster to meet me, planting a kiss on my lips. "Did you miss me?" she asks. I reply, "Do you even have to ask?"

I walk her to her car, and kiss her again feeling volts of energy surge though me like lighting.
"See you tonight around six-thirty p.m. or so?"
"Sounds perfect." I quickly kiss her again and watch her drive away. I get in my car, and I am off to pick up Jazz at the shopping center. Glad he has an interview and hoping so much he gets the job. I arrive at the shopping center and Jazz is waiting for me. He gets in the car looking bored, but who could blame him having to sit here and wait for three hours. I mean it was hard for me to be in class and wait to get out.

The Disturbed

"Hey man, sorry you had to wait so long. If I could have been here sooner I would have."

"Hey, no problem man, I am thankful for the ride. How was class?"

"Good, nice but slow. I couldn't wait to get out either."

"That's understandable, I mean you have no choice but to sit there, I guess I didn't either I suppose…we both laugh."

"There is a bus that runs down this street but I think it's once every two hours or so that is still a wait. Glad to be on the way home now.

We got back home although the drive seemed like an hour. The quietness during the drive home felt awkward, which was weird considering I had known Jazz all my life. One thing I was sure about him, he knew how to hold a grudge. I tried to crack a smile from Jazz on the way and it was pretty easy because he was excited about his upcoming interview. The thought of Lacy coming over excited me, and I am sure Jazz could see it written all over my face. I hoped he would find someone to date or hang-out with because he was alone most of the time other than the time we spent together at home or out. Jazz was always a loner, but he was really alone out here because there were no other people for miles, and the fact that he moved away from his family didn't help. Part of me felt bad, but part of me knew it was his own choice to come with me too. He talked to his family often, and I think sometimes he was more home sick than I was, and with good reason. I was expecting Lacy by six p.m., so I started to get ready, and clean up around the place a bit. I mean we are bachelors so this place needs some work. Sure, could use a woman's touch and again it made me miss Mom. I started on the dishes in the kitchen, and then went into my room to gather all of my dirty laundry off of the floor, made my bed, made sure there was toilet paper in the bathroom, the seat was down, and there was no toothpaste all over the sink from this morning. It was five-thirty; I hopped in the shower to wash off the day. When I got out I decided to give Lacy a call, and ask her what she wanted from the Chinese takeout, after all it would probably be an hour before our food arrived seeing I lived in the boonies. I asked Jazz if he wanted anything from the Chinese restaurant, and he said no, so I called in our order, and waited for Lacy. I saw head lights coming in the long driveway we had. I was hoping it was her, but it wasn't, it was a cop car. "What the hell?" I open the front door with a look of surprise, and hoped that there was not an issue.

"Good evening, I am Officer Finn. This here is Officer Dakota, we are in the area asking residents if they have seen or heard anything suspicious around these parts? It seems we have two residents missing from our city. We are trying to gather any possible information and make residents aware of our concerns to keep the community safe."

"Oh wow! I appreciate you coming by, but I have not been home much. However, the time I have been home I have not seen nor heard anything out of the ordinary anyway."

"Yes, well, we are not saying anything is wrong we are just taking precautions as part of our job."

"Oh yes, well sure, I completely understand. Thank you for coming out and keeping us informed, sure is appreciated." Just then Lacy drove up the driveway.

"Well, looks like you got company, we will get out of your hair. If you hear or see anything don't hesitate to call the station or 911 if you are in need, okay?"

"Sure thing, thank you!" Lacy gets out of her car and slowly walks to the front door as the cops are heading down the steps.

"Evening ma'am." One of the cops says before they both get in their car and drive off.

"Wow Derek, what was all that about? Is everything okay?"

"Yeah babe, everything is fine, I guess they are looking for two people is all and were asking if we had seen anything weird around here." I didn't want to make light of it but I didn't want Lacy to feel uncomfortable either. "They were just giving the residents in the area heads up on safety too." Then Lacy came out with it.

"Well you know what happened over here don't you? I guess it was somewhere close to this area anyway that a family was killed."

"Yeah, I found out after we moved in. It doesn't make me feel too comfortable, but we signed a lease for a year so I guess we are stuck here until then. I didn't know you knew and I wasn't about to freak you out with something like that."

"Aww thanks for thinking about me like that. That's one thing I love about you Derek." Did she just say love? I could feel my cheeks turn red with excitement.

I turn on the TV and get everything set up for our movie. We talk awhile then the doorbell rings "Food's here." "Yes!" Lacy says with excitement. Boy was I shocked when I tasted the Chinese food, it was the best I had ever had. I think what surprised me the most was that we were in the country now so I was not expecting it to be so good.

The Disturbed

"So, do you like The Lazy Chinese?"

"Oh yeah, that is one of my favorite places to order in from."

"Awesome, so I had a good idea huh?"

"Sure did." She says with that ear to ear smile I love so much.

We stare at each other the whole time we eat and talk about the unimportant things of the last week, and I never get bored of listening to her no matter what we talk about. She seemed to feel the same with me. We finish our dinner, I grab a cozy blanket from my room, and we cuddle up on the couch. She leans into me, and I pull her closer. This is the best feeling in the world, I think to myself. We both have a late class in the morning and I am scheduled to work tomorrow night so we have the whole night to ourselves. Lacy had been dropping hints that she wanted me, I mean really wanted me. There was no denying that I wanted her. We get about twenty minutes into the movie, and she leans her head back, and looks at me, smiles big then kisses me on the lips. I kiss her back even harder. She slightly turns around now half of her body facing me. She strokes the back of my neck gently. My hands move to her face, her nose to mine as I kiss her with intense passion. We both feel the passion that has been building for weeks now, and the love we feel for each other is flowing through us tonight as we give in to our passions. We kiss for what seemed to be an hour, loving every minute of it. Putting her lips closer to mine, she whispers "I want you Derek." and I knew what she meant. I scoop her up in my arms and carry her to my room still kissing her. I lay her gently on the bed, lock the door to my room, and dim the lights. I lay next to her, kissing her, allowing myself to feel all the passion that had been stored up. Now knowing she wanted me just as much as I wanted her. We undress each other slowly, but seductively until our bodies lay next to each other. Our breathing starts to get rapid and I want to taste her. She is sweet just as I knew she would be and so ready for me. I please her, giving her what she wants…she screams with pleasure and I feel her nails dig into my shoulders. It is such a turn-on. I kiss her as she screams looking into my eyes. I enter her slowly; she whines with pleasure "Yes," she says to me as she pulls me into her deeper. I plan to please her for a long time, and place her hands above her head holding them in place with mine. She does not resist me, in fact she wants it. Our passion turns wild. The two of us together is like fire. In the heat of our passion, I pick her up off the bed taking her to the wall, gently leaning her against the wall as I thrust deep inside her. She screams with pleasure…"Take me Derek!" Take her I do, in every position I can possibly imagine. As we make mad passionate love I can't help but think how much it feels

The Disturbed

like the first time. I know she is pleased with me because her moans tell me how pleased she is as we love on each other for hours. The night could not have been more perfect, and I could not feel more loved. I had never felt more loved by a girl in all my life, nor had I even loved a girl so much. What we have is magical and I was not going to let it get away, ever.

We wake up in each other's arms as the sun comes up. I kiss her on the forehead she smiles back at me with that beautiful smile of hers.

"Are you hungry, would you like some coffee or orange juice?"

"Some orange juice sounds great, what if we grab a bite to eat out?"

"Sounds great to me, let me get that orange juice for you."

I think she was feeling a bit of what I was feeling with Jazz being home and in the kitchen. I walked out to the kitchen and told Jazz I would be back to pick him up as soon as I was done and to be ready so he would not be late. I hated to sound like his mother, but I was just trying to be helpful. Lacy and I enjoyed a nice breakfast, after I walked her to her car, thanked her for a beautiful evening, kissing gently then went our separate ways. We would see each other in a couple of hours in class so that was a nice thought. We both had class in the morning, then I had a therapist appointment, course then it was off to work for my night shift. Lacy and I had been doing some studying so I felt pretty good about my classes and the midterm coming-up. I felt like I was ready to leave the gas station job too, find something better. I thought about switching my classes to night classes next semester, so I could find a better paying full-time job, as well as more enjoyable one. I mean the gas station was okay, but I would rather move around a lot more than be stuck to one seat the whole shift. It was something Lacy and I had talked about, she agreed on switching next semester.

Jazz was waiting for me at home so I rushed back to pick him up. It was his day to shine and I was hoping he would get the job. I got home and Jazz was ready which was cool because I also had to get to class.

"Hey man, you look sharp!"

"Thanks, it's just a supermarket job but I want to do something during the day ya know? Plus, it should give me some money to save for a car so I can go back to school in a few months too."

It was good to hear Jazz talk about school again, and have some goals. Maybe he had been a bit depressed

The Disturbed

after the move, being so stuck out here; I mean it is a culture-shock for sure.

"That sounds like a great plan to me bro. Next semester I will be changing my schedule to go to school at night so I can get a better job that lets me move around a bit more you know. If you like I could put in a good word for you if you would be interested in the gas station job as well. I mean you would save a lot faster man."

"Hey that sounds great...Yes, let me know when you will be leaving okay that sounds great. Can you bring me an application from work?"
"Sure thing, bring you one tonight."
"Sweet! Thanks Derek for helping me out man."
"No problem, that's what friends are for, I am always here for you bro. I think getting out will help you be able to meet people too. I mean you could use a girlfriend." I say as I laughed.
"Okay Derek, I don't need any help in that area man. Back off a bit, will ya."
"Come on man sorry. Just joking with ya. Sure, no problem, I'll lighten up." As I'm still laughing at his reaction. We have joked around like this since we were kids but Jazz has sure been on the tight-ass side of things lately.

"Lighten up man, don't get all tense before your interview, I was just fucking around man. Hey, for what it's worth I hope you get the job today."

"Thanks, I feel pretty good about it."

We get to the grocery store where Jazz is having his interview this morning, Jazz gets out of the car looking a bit nervous.

"Hey, I will take that bus home today okay. It only comes like twice a day but I will get home sooner if I do that than if I wait here."

"Okay man, see you at home. Hey and break a leg. Late"

"Late man!" He shuts the door and I drive off I almost feel relieved or freed in some way of having to pick him up. I have ten minutes to get to class, but I will make it, I mean it's the class I have with Lacy, I have to make it.

I walk in to class with one minute to spare. Lacy looks at me with a big grin, God that smile and those eyes. I am in love with this girl, I think she is the one. I sit down noticing I was staring right at her the whole time I was thinking all of this. The instructor begins the class but it's impossible to concentrate with her anywhere near me. She seems to have the same problem as we secretly pass notes back and forth trying not to be seen by the instructor. Every time she gets my note she giggles, thank god, the instructor is loud. The two-hour class ends, and we meet each

The Disturbed

other outside. I think we are both still love struck from last night as we stare into one another eyes. We spend a few minutes together than I am off to the therapist to check in and possibly get a refill. I mean the meds have been working a bit I guess, I am not having the delusions as much as I was, but I am also a lot happier now than I was. Although, I have never shared with her about my delusions, nor have we talked about the reasons behind my medication except for sleep. I think it was out of fear I didn't disclose in detail everything although, I knew one day I would have to open-up about all of it.

I arrive at the therapy office and sit to be called back. The office is not as modern as the one back in California, but it's still nice. I like Dr. Wright too, she makes me feel comfortable even though I have only seen her once. Lacy knows I come to therapy and thinks it's always good to learn more about one's self in general. I was pretty worried when I had to tell her I even go to therapy, but I wanted her to know all of me if she was going to be in my life, except for the delusions. I felt it had to be the right time to bring that up.

Dr. Wright comes to the lobby.
"Are you ready to come back?"
"Sure, thank you." We get to her office and she closes the door.

"How has everything been going Derek?"

"Well, actually very good, the medications I have been on seem to be working for me so far. Although, I am thinking it could be because I have relocated as well. I am thinking of changing my class schedule to evening so I can get a better job. I mean I enjoy the gas station job somewhat, but I need more excitement I guess, I get bored easy there."

"That is totally understandable Derek and makes good sense. I am glad to hear that the medications are also helping you. So, you haven't had any more delusions at all?"

"No, I had one when I walked home from the gas station one night after lending my car out to Jazz, the guy I live with. I chalked that up to anxiety though because I never had one after that, I mean so far anyway."

"Well, that does sound like the meds are working well with you. So, what else is going on in your life?"

"I have a new girlfriend and she is just wonderful."

"Oh really, how long have you two been together?"

"Only three weeks but I feel like I have known her for years. I mean I feel more comfortable with her than I do with Jazz lately. Maybe because Jazz and I have been having some issues with respect and I would say jealousy."

"Tell me about that."

"Well, remember what I said about my loaning out my car to him for a day and me having to walk home. Well, I had to walk home because Jazz didn't come get me because he fell asleep on the coach and forgot to pick me up. So, I had to walk five miles down that long, dark street I live off of."

"So, how did that make you feel?"

"To be completely honest it pissed me off. I mean it was completely disrespectful and I told him afterward that he couldn't borrow my car again. I am not sure if that was too harsh, but me having to walk home after working my shift I think that was something a best friend just doesn't do. Jazz has been acting a bit funny about my new girlfriend too, well jealous anyway which really messes with my head. I want to come home and have it feel peaceful where I live you know?"

"Again Derek, that's completely understandable and not unreasonable at all. You are doing a great job, and you should expect those around you to do the same or at least respect your own efforts. What is Jazz doing as far as getting a job to help and contribute around the house?"

"He had an interview today so that is good and I am still trying to help him out as much as I can until he gets on his feet as well. He says he wants to go back to school after he gets settled in his job, and gets more familiar with the area. I can understand that because it must be hard leaving his family and little sister and stuff too you know. We also just found out that we live in a house that is very close to where a whole family was killed; actually, it practically happened in our backyard. It surprised me how Jazz really didn't have a response to it when I told him. It sure freaked me out for a while though."

"That is interesting. How are you feeling about it now?"

"I am okay I guess, I mean not much I can do about it now that I am in a lease there now as well so, I just tried to do some research on what happened. I guess to gain some peace in my heart about living here."

"Now that shows a great deal of caring, and concern for others, and just what had happened in general Derek. I am proud of you for doing that, I am sure it had to be very hard to learn about what had happened there, and the details of those who died so close to the place you call home. As far as Jazz is concerned sounds like he has to find his own way, but it sure is good of you to be there for him like you are as a good friend would be."

"Yeah, thank you, it's been hard but it all seems to be working out."

"Well, great, I think you will do great in your new job as well. So, how are your classes going, your grades staying up?"

"Yeah, for the most part, I mean I could mess around a bit less, but having Lacy in one of my classes doesn't help matters much. I am excited to see what the future holds with her though, that's for sure."

"Nice, very nice, I am happy for you Derek, I really am. Look our time is almost up, but I would like to keep

The Disturbed

you on the same medications for now and give it some more time and see how things go, if that's okay with you?

"Yes, sounds good to me."

"Okay great. So, I will write you a prescription for two months and seeing that you are doing so well I will see you in two months unless you need to come in sooner for any reason. If so you can just give me a call and I will get you in here."

"Perfect."

"Okay, here you go Derek; it was nice to chat with you again and take care of yourself and remember to get rest while you are taking care of all these other things as well okay."

"Sure thing Dr. Wright. Thank you."

"Thank you, Derek, see you in a couple of months."

I walk out of Dr. Wrights office relieved that I don't have to come back for a couple of months and glad that the medications are working. Over all I am feeling pretty happy with my life. I start heading home wondering how Jazz's interview went. Just then my phone rings, it's Lacy.

"Hey sweetie! How did the therapy appointment go?"

"Great, thanks babe; she said I didn't have to come back for a couple of months because I'm doing so well. I guess the meds are really helping too."

"Wonderful hon, that's really great news."

"Yeah I thought so. She did seem a bit surprised by what I told her about how Jazz responded to learning about the family being killed so close to where we live. She didn't act like anything was wrong with that she just took notice I guess."

"Yeah, well we all respond differently to different things babe, so maybe that was just his way of dealing with it. On a positive note though, you have one less appointment to go to for a few months anyway, right?"

"Right!"

"So where are you now?"

"I am heading home for a shower and some dinner. Where you at?"

"Just got home from the store with Mom, cooking dinner now. Speaking of cooking dinner would you like to come over for dinner Thursday night? I have been meaning to ask you, but I know you work nights now. I was thinking if you like you could come have dinner and meet Mom your next night off. What do you think?"

"Oh Lac, that sounds amazing. It's a date next Thursday night, I am yours. All night if you want me." I add a shy laugh to the conversation to take the heaviness off of what I just said.

"Oh yes! I can't wait for you to be all mine, all night."

My heart beats faster with excitement and desire for her. This is one amazing woman and I am not letting her get away.

The Disturbed

"Babe, I have to let you go for now, I am home, going to hop in the shower and eat some dinner."
"Okay sweetie, call me later if you'd like, mwah."
"I will, mwah!"

I walk in the door and see Jazz sitting on the couch.
"Hey man, how did it go today?"
"Oh, hey Derek, it went pretty good man, I mean I feel good about how the interview went. I am hoping I get a call back from them. I also have the application for the gas station for you to hand in if you still plan on leaving."
"Yeah sure man, get it and I will take it in tonight"
Jazz's phone rings.

"Hello?"
"Hello, may I speak to Jazz Kingston please?"
"Yes, this is he. How can I help you?"
"This is the Wellington Grocery Store; we wanted to know if you are still interested in working for us as a clerk?"
"Yes, I sure am. When would you like me to start?"
"Can you come in this next Wednesday nine a.m. for an orientation, and after that you would be able to start the following Thursday?"
"Absolutely, I will be there at nine a.m. on Wednesday, is there anything else I need to know or bring?"

"Just make sure you bring your identification card and social security card with you on Wednesday morning and that should be all you need."
"Great, thank you for calling."
"You are very welcome Jazz and congratulations."
"Thank you again, see you Wednesday."
"Great! Goodnight."
"Goodnight."

Jazz hangs-up the phone and gives a yell "Yes! I got the store job."
"Sweet! Man…That was fast. Great job Jazz!"
"I know right! I am stoked man. Now I can save for a damn car."
"High-five man. When do you start?"
"I go in on Wednesday for orientation and start on Thursday. By the way, can you give me a ride maybe on both days Derek, just until I get a route figured out?"
"Hey, no problem, I got you, don't even worry about it man, whatever you need. I am psyched for you. Good news all day, it's been a good day indeed. I don't have to see my therapist for a few months because she says I am doing really well. So that was great news for me today too. Hey, I am hopping in the shower then making some dinner, then it's off to work for me."
"Alright, oh and great news Derek, good to hear you get a break from the therapist."

The Disturbed

"Thanks."

I get done with my shower and dinner then I am off to the glorious gas station. "Hey Jazz, you got that application for me to turn in for you?"
"Sure, right here, hey thanks again Derek."
"Not a problem, that's what friends are for right?"
"Yeah, but I really appreciate this man."
"Hey, remember we are in this together. I will make sure to turn this in tonight."

I head out the door to work. It's nice to see Jazz in a better mood. I will call Lacy and tell her the good news on my break. I can't get her off my mind. I turned in the application Jazz gave me when I got in to work. Sam seemed to like it a lot; I think he also trusted my judgement as well. I told him I was not leaving until the fifteenth of next month. He told me not to worry my job was here anytime I wanted it, and what a great job I had done the whole time working for him. He also mentioned how sad he was to see me go, but I knew I had to move on, make a better life in the future and especially to be able to pay for school. But there was also the fact that I was bored at this job, it was just time to see what else came my way.

I get halfway through my shift and I hear something in the back of the small store-room of the gas station.

I walk back there slowly to find out what was going on. I was a bit nervous especially being there all alone so late at night, but I had been here for a while now and had never had any problems before. I peek around the corner and I see the light from the street-light shining down on the floor. "Hello?" I say out loud but there is no answer nor movement. The back door is wide open and Sam has never left that door unlocked, especially during the night shift. I walk to the door feeling white as a ghost wondering if someone is in the room including that faceless fuck that has freaked me out for almost two years now. I grab my cell and give Sam a quick call to make sure he locked the door in which he confirms to me he did. Then how the hell did it get open? Not only how, but why? Feeling really concerned I call Jazz who has always been there for me as my support, he doesn't pick-up. I wasn't going to call Lacy but I needed her now, bad. I ring Lacy and she doesn't pick-up either so I decide to get to the door as fast as I can to lock it up. I grab a large flash-light and head to the door ready for anything. I get to the door, close, and lock it, looking around for anything out of the ordinary, but nothings moved. Breathing a sigh of relief, I go back to the front before I get a customer needing gas. I sit down and bury my head in my arms for a moment taking in a few deep breaths. I look up to see if I have any customers and I see him. My body goes numb knowing I can't

The Disturbed

reach anyone at the moment and I am scared shitless. I watch him for as long as my eyes will allow me to. He is walking away from the gas station in the direction of my home. He looks back and smirks at me again with the lipless grin, it looks like he is wearing a mask, but I can't tell. He has to be, I think to myself because how does he breathe. I shake my head and he is gone. Fuck! Am I having delusions again? What the hell is going on with me now? Maybe I am stressed about changing jobs or something. I have been doing so well, and feel so damn happy how can this be happening to me again? I try and work on some breathing exercises I learned with Dr. Searian two years ago, it seems to help for a bit but I am still a mess. Maybe I am trying to figure out too much all at once in my life? All of a sudden I feel very relieved, I will be leaving this job on the fifteenth of next month, it is definitely time for me to go before I lose my mind. I calm down enough to try, and give Lacy another call this time she answers, but I can't tell her about what just happened. I want her to think I am doing well and all is okay. I mean I know it is all well, but I don't want to lose her is all.

"Hey babe, how are you doing?"
    "Great! I'm missing you. How is your night going?"
    "It's going alright hon, I can't wait until tomorrow to spend time with you though, you amazing woman you."

"Derek, you are the amazing one babe, and I can't wait to be with you either. I may just kidnap you in your own house and take advantage of you."

"Like I would put up a fight, right?" Feeling so glad she answered her phone because I sure needed this calm connection right now.

"So, you are still coming for dinner tomorrow first, right?"

"Oh yes, I wouldn't miss it babe."

"Sweet, miss you and love you. I will let you get back to work, but I can't wait to see you tomorrow. Have sweet dreams of me babe."

"Oh, you better believe I will and I miss you and love you too. Can't wait to see you tomorrow hon. Have a great night, see you at school in the morning okay."

"Sounds great, goodnight babe."

"Goodnight."

I hang up the phone feeling relieved just from hearing her voice. Man do I thank God for her, she is special that's for sure. I have a half hour to go before my shift ends, and all I can think about is getting home. But in the back of my mind I wonder if I will encounter that faceless fuck again. I truly don't know what to call him so I guess that's the fucker's name. I am hoping that these delusions go away completely so I never have to talk about them with Lacy. It scares me to think about

The Disturbed

sharing that part of my life with her and wondering if she will still want me. It's time to go and I get my stuff together as I start to close-up. I know Jazz will be good here because shit doesn't get to him like it does me. I guess if it was all happening to him, he may view it all a bit different, maybe, who knows. Jazz is very different than I am in many ways and this is one of them. My shift ended, but I am not feeling too great about the drive home. I keep envisioning him throwing himself in front of the car to get me to stop. Maybe I have watched too many horror flicks, who knows, but I can't help but wonder where the hell he walked to? I pull out of the gas station driveway and drive semi-slow down my street. Then I start to think how does this guy know where the fuck I'm working? Has he been watching me this whole time? I wonder if maybe he had a car hiding in the dark or something, my thoughts were racing. I keep driving about a mile down the road that leads to my house and I see a car parked on the side of the road in the dark. I can't help but think that is him, but as I pass by I don't see anyone in the car. I only live another five and half miles down the street, I start to panic thinking the worst. I give Jazz a call again to see if he will answer now.

"Jazz, hey man, you asleep?"

"Nope just sitting here thinking about my orientation appointment tomorrow, I guess I am a bit nervous about it."

"Oh man, don't stress you will do great for sure. You got this in the bag, man. Hey, I was just calling to check on you because I saw that guy again man. You know that faceless guy? And he was walking down the street that leads to our house."

"Wow, really? You okay man?"

"Yeah I am good but glad to be on my way home. Where were you about two hours ago man, I tried to call you because the back-door here was open and I was freaking out. It was nothing but after I locked the door I saw that faceless fuck again man. I almost called the cops, but I don't want them to say it's my meds or something you know."

"Yeah, that's understandable for sure. Well, at least you are alright and on your way home, huh."

"Yeah, thanks for being there man, see you in a few. Late."

"Late."

I finally got home without another incident but of course feeling overwhelmed. Jazz asks me how I was doing when I walked in the door but I didn't have much of a reply at the time; I just wanted to retreat to my room for some solitude. I took my meds and it was off to bed for me, I could not wait to see Lacy in the morning.

I got up early and headed to school. I could not wait to see Lacy anymore, the night had been long enough

The Disturbed

without her, she had a way of calming me within like nothing, and no one else could. Lacy looked beautiful when I greeted her at class. I was excited to go to dinner at her house tonight and I could tell she was as well. Jazz started his new job today and Sam had also called him this morning for a job interview, and man was he excited about that, two jobs lined up in one week. Pretty damn good if you ask me. I was glad things were looking up for him, it was sad to say maybe, but it took the guilt off of me, making me able to enjoy my life freely now with Lacy knowing he was not just always sitting at home. I couldn't wait until he bought a car too so he could maybe get back in school or have some type of dating life. This was my night off, and I intended to make it a good one with my girl by my side. Class ended early because we had finals coming up in a week and our instructor thought it would be good to study some uploaded presentations. I was glad because it gave me more time with Lacy.

It was time to get ready for dinner at her house, I was nervous but ready. She came over to pick me up. I get in the car leaning over to give her a kiss. We get to her house, I meet her parents, and I can see why Lacy is such a beautiful person. I think Lacy's parents like me, but I can't tell yet, I know her Mom can sure cook. We have a wonderful time at dinner, I help clean-up, then I thanked them for a wonderful evening and we say our good byes. I'm so glad Lacy brought me because I would feel very awkward with her not having a reason to leave with me so late. I mean she had spent the night away from home already, but now that I was face to face with her parents there sure was a bit more pressure. It did feel a bit awkward leaving with her knowing she was going to spend the night at my house, but I guess her parents knew she was a grown woman who was able to make a decision on her own. Of course, this didn't help me as her boyfriend, feeling the awkwardness of taking their daughter overnight. Lacy kissed her Mom and said goodnight to both her Mom, and Dad then we got in the car to drive to my house. As soon as we got in the car I had to know from Lacy's point of view anyway, what her parents thought about me. I was relieved when Lacy shared with me that her Mom pulled her aside in the kitchen and told her she really liked me a lot, she thought I was good for her. I felt like I wanted to jump out of my seat I was so excited. I loved this girl and I wanted her parents to like me so badly. We pulled into the driveway of my house and I couldn't wait to be alone with her again. This time we put a movie on in my room and cuddled while it started. I could tell she wanted me again and I was going to give her what she wanted. We made love for hours, until we saw the sun coming-up, taking small breaks in between. It had been a long week and she showed me how long. We could not get enough

The Disturbed

of each other's intense passion and I loved it. Finally falling asleep about six a.m. we slept until around two in the afternoon. It was a day to just be together and do nothing. I knew I had to start looking for a new job, but I also knew I had at least two weeks to do so. I was not worried about finding something here at all, I guess I was feeling aligned with the stars as if something would fall into my lap.

Lacy and I go into the kitchen to get something to eat, and Jazz had just gotten home from his new job. He sure seemed happier and more content which was nice to see. It didn't seem to bother him as much this time that Lacy was here which was also nice. Jazz asked me the in's and out's about the gas station job, hoping to make himself more ready for it. I was thinking about looking for a job possibly delivering hay or something like that where I could be out an about while at the same time be my own boss. It was also something that Lacy had suggested for me to look into as an idea for my day job. In fact, she already had a person she wanted me to meet. His name was Mr. RJ Burns. He owned a small company of delivery trucks and delivered to all the surrounding cities in Alabama. It was late in the afternoon but I decided to give him a call. I guess you could say I was eager to make some much-needed changes soon. I pick up the phone and Lacy dials.

"It's ringing."

"Hello, Burns Hay."

"Hello, may I speak to Mr. RJ Burns please?"

"This is he, who may I ask is speaking?"

"Hello, Mr. Burns, my name is Derek Holson. A friend of mine named Lacy Anderson referred me to you for a possible job delivering hay bales to the local surrounding cities and I am very much interested, sir."

"Oh yes, I have known Lacy for years. I just happen to be hiring as well. How long have you and Lacy known each other?"

"Almost six months now sir, and if anyone knows me it would be Lacy. I just moved here from California, I currently work at the Wellington Corner Gas Station, but I'm looking to change my hours and find a job I would really enjoy, that gets me out and about a bit more. I also have a great reference with the owner of the gas station if you would like their contact information sir."

"Well I can certainly say, I trust Lacy's judgment and I would be glad to give you an interview next Thursday about ten a.m. in the morning if that works for you."

"Oh yes sir, that works fine for me, I will bring my resume and the contact information to my current employer for you as well next Thursday at ten a.m."

"Sounds good Derek, see you then."

"Thank you, sir, for this opportunity, I greatly appreciate it. See you next week."

The Disturbed

"Alright, next week it is, good day Derek and if you would.... tell Lacy I said hello."

"Will do sir, bye now"

I hang-up the phone and let out a yell of excitement that could have been heard in California, hypothetically speaking anyway. Lacy joins in with a scream that was so cute. I grab her and roll her on her back kissing her passionately.

"Thank you, babe, for hooking me up with Mr. Burns. I love you immensely."

"You are more than welcome babe, and I love you more."

"Oh yeah!" I grab her, pinning her down with one hand and tickling her with my other hand as I kiss her neck. I felt so connected to her. I just knew we were going to be together forever, and I planned to make sure of it, as much as it was in my power anyway. I let her up from my love pin, we both laugh at the fun we are having, and the good news.

"See sometimes all you have to do is just believe Derek, and good things do pour into your lap." This is another thing I loved so much about Lacy; she always believed the very best in every situation no matter what it was about. She sure was a strength to me that's for certain.

CHAPTER 6

Disturbed

Lacy and I planned to spend the day together watching movies and eating all day. She made me her favorite nacho recipe and I made my famous spaghetti for a late lunch before I had to go to work, which by the way I was not looking forward to. After what had happened last Wednesday night I worked, I could not wait to leave that job. What was interesting was Jazz could not wait to start that job which was already his according to Sam the owner. I mean I could totally understand him wanting to make more money to be able to get himself a car and then there was the fact that he was not dating anyone nor had a life outside of work. But I was sure spooked to work there now but he seemed cool with it, which kind of threw me. Of course, he had never seen the faceless fuck before so I guess that made a lot more sense not having experienced what I had experienced first-hand. It was getting late and time for Lacy to head home and me to go to my night job and I was dreading it. I wished I could take her with me because I felt so comfortable with her near me, but I knew that was not in my reality. We said our goodbyes, I shut her car door kissed her, and off she went. She was coming over tomorrow, I had told Sam I needed a day off last week so it was another night for Lacy and me to be alone together. I think that's what was getting me through this night as I walked into the gas station booth once again with those dreaded memories from last Wednesday night. God this place spooked me out, I felt scarred for life at least working here anyway. As the night went on I could not get what had happened out of my mind. I tried to listen to music, do a bit of studying for my final, but I kept going back to the thoughts of that fucking night. It was so bad at times I felt like calling Sam and telling him I just can't work here anymore, but I had responsibilities. I mean I had my school loans which I was saving money for so I could be ahead of the payments, so I tried as hard as I could not to call. I was glad to have tomorrow off; I knew I needed it bad, even if it was to give myself

The Disturbed

time away from here for a while or as much as possible before I was able to leave for good.

I was able to get through the night without any more mind games going on in my head. Studying for the final I think helped me a lot in taking my mind off of the fact that I was still at work, the night sure did seem to drag on though. Tonight, I have off and Lacy will be here to keep me company so I know it will be an amazing time as always. I decided to get some laundry done and clean up around the house. I had been seeing Lacy for a few months now, but always felt the need to impress her whenever I could, even if it was just having a clean pad. Lacy and I went over our schedule changes to make sure they were the same so we could spend as much time at school as possible. I loved passing notes in class like high school kids and send sexy gestures across the room to her when the instructor wasn't looking. Lacy and I had fun doing whatever we were doing at that moment, she made life fun and I made life fun for her no matter if we were sitting there together in quietness. It was always peaceful; even if we disagreed we always came back to our tranquil centered same energy. She was my soulmate and I just knew she was the one I would marry someday.

Monday came and it was finally time for finals. I was glad because I just wanted to get them over with, as did Lacy.

I was also excited to change our schedules to nights so we could see each other more on the days we did not have school after work. It was a grueling hour for the final, but we managed to get through it pretty fast, well finishing with five minutes to spare anyway. I think I did pretty good, Lacy said she felt she did pretty well on it as well. We were sure glad it was over; I mean I had enough on my mind with the interview coming-up for that job I really wanted. At least there was a small break in between registering for classes. I wanted to focus on changing the schedule, getting everything else ready as far as work was concerned so I could spend more time with Lacy and handle the demands of the class work.

I had to work tonight and Sam had asked me to start training Jazz for the job I had been doing for the week to make sure he would be able to do the job without any assistance. Jazz is a pretty smart guy so I really didn't think he would have any problems picking it up quick, it wasn't hard that's for sure. I mean the hardest thing about working the gas station was staying awake the whole shift because it would get quiet and slow. There were some safety things I had to make sure he knew about so it was not just sit in a chair and take people's money; he needed to know what to do in case anything went wrong on a pump or with the gasoline as well which was always in the back of my mind. I am not sure if it was my anxiety or what, but I would always think what if this or what if that when it came to shit like the gas station going up in flames or something. I think that is why Lacy evens me out so much, she is the optimist in everything I seem to panic about. Jazz, well he did not scare easy at all, that was one trait I wish I had inherited more of from my dad. Lately Jazz has been asking a lot of questions about Lacy and I. At first, I didn't think anything of it, but it is starting to bother me just a bit because they're personal questions. I wondered if he could hear us in the bedroom or if he was just bored and was trying to find things to talk about. He knows I love her a lot, and think the world about her, but he would ask questions like "So, are you and Lacy doing the wild-thing often?" I mean, I know we are guys and stuff but I found that to be a bit weird, almost as if he was jealous of her spending the night all the time or at least as much as she could. But, it was not all about sex for us; we loved to be together doing whatever no matter how boring it might have seemed to anyone else. I would try and change the subject as much as he would bring it up, and it seemed to drive the knife in harder with him. I finally asked him if he had a thing for Lacy, which of course he denied from the get go. He was never disrespectful to her or me but it all seemed to close for comfort knowing he was just in the other room all the time and probably heard us having sex when she stayed with me. But it wasn't like he was going to shut us up. Lacy was wild and well, she made me wild and I loved it.

It was time for me to get to the gas station and finish this final week. I tapped on Jazz's door to see if he was ready to go with me for the training tonight. I only had through the weekend to get him ready and Thursday was my day off.

"Hey Jazz, you ready to go train with me tonight man?"

"Oh shit! Yeah man, hold on a minute let me get dressed really quick. I forgot I had to train with you today because the new job at the store has got me drained. I will be right out okay."

"Yeah man, no problem we have about twenty minutes before I take-over the shift and we need driving time so let's go man."

"I hear ya, I am on it."

Jazz comes bolting out of his room ready to go train for his second job, while I am hoping all the while he does not flake on Sam because he is not used to having two jobs yet. But, he has always been responsible when it came to important things and never flaked much on anything, which is a good thing. I would never want to disappoint Sam with referring him, when Sam has always been such a great boss to me.

The Disturbed

We are on the drive to the station and Jazz starts with the questions.

"So, I guess Sam gives you the keys to the place seeing that you are the only one there to open and close the place and are there all night, right?"

"Yep, he does and puts a lot of trust in you to keep the place safe too." I try to focus on the fact that he is taking on my responsibility in a round-about way as to not offend him, but let him know as a friend I expect him to do his part here, as we pull up.

"Don't worry Derek, I got you on this man, I won't let you down. I mean I understand what you are trying to say. I got in here because I know you and you don't want me to fuck it up. I get it okay."

"Okay, thanks man."

We get out of the car and I show him around the place, focusing on some important things first like where all the emergency switches are in case anything were to happen during his shift. Then we go inside to do the paperwork of the night and show him the ropes on the cash register, which he's already pretty familiar with being a check-out clerk at the grocery store he works at. All in all, it was a pretty slow night but Jazz was able to get familiar with the place at least. I answered some questions he had and he seemed to be feeling calm about taking over here. Lacy and I had just finished our finals, so we had a couple of weeks off from school before we would be starting back up again. We had to register for our new classes in the next two weeks so we planned to change our schedule this Thursday in the morning before my interview. I was glad next Sunday would be my last day at the gas station; I sure didn't feel comfortable there. I felt confident in Jazz's ability to take over; I mean I have known the guy for years and trusted him with pretty much everything. But, I was still hoping he would find a girl to date to help him get his mind off of me and Lacy's doings. I know when you are in high school you tend to share everything with your buddies, but I was grown now and this was personal to me and I wanted it to stay that way. I loved Lacy with a love I had never known before and I was not about to let even an eighteen-year friendship come in between that.

It was Thursday and I was excited. I had been waiting for this day because it meant change for Lacy and I. We had planned to get our classes changed in the morning so I could have time to get ready for my interview with Mr. Burns. I was also excited because Lacy was coming over and planned to stay the night, which was always fun because we were like teenagers, you know popcorn, movie, cooking munchies, and lots of love-making, can't forget the cuddling. We both got up early; Lacy

The Disturbed

came to get me then we headed to the school to make the schedule changes. It wasn't that hard due to the fact that we were in between classes so all we had to really do was inform student affairs that we would be changing to evening classes. Even though the school was not full they still wanted the students to make changes as soon as possible in order for the school to be prepared for the changes in students to semesters and classes, which was completely understandable. We got to the school and it took maybe an hour for both of us to change our schedules. Lacy was changing her schedule at her job as well; it amazed me how smooth everything was going with her and me. We were all set to register for night classes in about two weeks, now it was time to get ready for my job interview. I sure wanted this job. It was perfect for what I needed and exactly what I wanted to do at the time. I had gotten ready for the interview before we went to the school knowing that it would be close to ten a.m. by the time we got done there and I was able to head to the interview. I let Lacy stay at the house while I went to the interview, after all she was going to spend the night again, and I didn't see the point in her going home when she had clothes here already.

I find the address for, "Burns Hay" which was the company I was hoping to work for. I walk in and greet the receptionist at the desk.

"Hello, good morning, I have an interview with Mr. RJ Burns this morning at ten a.m."
   "Very nice. Might I ask what your name is please?"
   "Yes, Derek Holson."
   "Okay, thank you Mr. Holson, please have a seat I'll let him know you are here."
   "Thank you."

My anxiety is through the roof right now as I sit and wait for the man who basically holds my future in his hands. I mean I could look for other options but my heart is pretty much set on working here, plus I am feeling really optimistic about the interview because he has known Lacy for so long. Just seems like where I am meant to be right now. I look up from watching myself rubbing my thumbs together and I see a short gray-haired man walking in my direction.

"Derek?"
   "Yes sir!"
   "Hello Derek, I'm Mr. Burns, glad to see ya. Come back this way where we can chat a bit."

I follow him back to his office which feels much like a home and he offers me a seat. I sit down and wait for him to speak.
   "So, Derek, tell me a bit about yourself."

The Disturbed

"Well, I am originally from Big Bear, California. I moved here to get away from the city and work on my Master's degree in Criminal Justice here in Alabama. I have worked at Wellington Corner Gas Station since I arrived here in Alabama about six months ago now and I have to say I love it here."

"So, Derek, tell me, how did you come to meet Lacy?"

"Well, I had just arrived in town moving here to Alabama with a childhood friend Jazz, who is now my room-mate. We saw Lacy on the side of the road having car trouble, and offered to help. Then I found out she was going to the same college I was about to attend, and the rest is history."

"Well, that was certainly nice of you to stop and help her after a long drive in, I like your character Derek. That is one of the things I look for here when I hire someone. You may be thinking this is not your average interview, but I am not your average employer either. I have known Lacy for many years, her parents are very good friends of mine, so to be honest, I can truly say I trust Lacy's judgement in character as well. Why is it you are leaving the gas station, and desire to work for me?"

"When I arrived here I was just looking for something close to home and school to pay the bills, and get settled here. After I met Lacy, I decided to change schedules so I could work day jobs to possibly make more money and go to school at night. Lacy, and I pretty much have the same idea when it comes to the future, meaning we both want to work days and continue our education at night."

"Very nice, it seems you both have great plans for yourselves and are headed in the right direction indeed."

"Thank you, Mr. Burns."

"Derek, I also would be honored if you would come work for me. How does fifty hours a week Monday through Friday sound at twelve dollars an hour to start, with some overtime on occasions, but I will also try to keep your schooling in mind when adding hours?"

"That sounds amazing to me Mr. Burns' and I appreciate it greatly."

"Okay then, when can you start?"

"How does next Monday sound?"

"Perfect! We will start you next Monday. I will have a guy take you around for the first week and show you how we go about our deliveries then you will be on your own."

"I am very excited! Thank you, Mr. Burns I can't wait to tell Lacy the great news."

I get up from my seat and shake Mr. Burns hand, thanking him again for the job with a huge grin on my face, of course. Saying good bye to the receptionist on my way out, I can't stop smiling. I mean this is exactly what I wanted and my life seemed to be exactly where I wanted it to be. I started to reflect on how I had made the decision to move here and how it seems to be the best

The Disturbed

decision I had ever made in my life. I could not wait to tell Lacy. Now I also had more amazing news for Mom as well. In a rush to get home I quickly stop at the local grocery store for some milk and other light groceries needed for tonight's dinner. I passed the display of flowers and I just had to get Lacy a dozen roses. I had never gotten her anything like that before, I sure felt now was an appropriate time to do so. I so appreciated her for all her help and love during our whole relationship thus far and had to show her somehow.

Just as I arrive home pulling up in the driveway my phone rings caller ID says: Lacy... "Yes!" I yell with excitement...

"Hey babe! Guess what?"

"Ummm, you got the job?"

"Yes! I got the job hon and the hours are perfect."

"Congratulations babe, I knew you would get in there and it would be perfect for you. Hey, I am still coming over tonight okay, I just have to run by the store with Mom first before I head over there. How does six-thirty p.m. sound?"

"That sounds great love; we can celebrate when you get here too, I am making dinner for you this time. Does spaghetti, salad, and garlic bread sound good to you? My Mom taught me a few things in the kitchen before I left. Oh, and I picked-up some Champagne too."

"Oh my gosh, that sounds so good babe, I can't wait!"

"Sweet, me either, I love you, see you when you get here."

"Okay, I love you too, see you then mwah!"

I started the dinner as soon as I got cleaned up and by the time I was done the house smelled like a damn restaurant. "God I'm good!" Then like I always do before Lacy comes over, I decided to clean-up the pad a bit. I could not remove the smile from my face knowing that now was the beginning of our future. I mean, I was thinking now I could maybe ask her to marry me. We had about a year and a half to go in college and we both had good jobs now, I pondered the thought of what she would say if I did ask her. Was it too soon? Was she ready for a commitment like that right now, at least an engagement? As I picked-up around the house I thought about all of this and how much I loved her, I really loved her. This was the one Mom had to meet. This was the one who would have my children. This was the only one I could see myself with for the rest of my life and I hoped she felt the same as I did way deep down inside. I would be trying to apply for the local Sheriff's department here after I got at least half way done with my degree, but having the new job delivering the hay was perfect to get me where I wanted to go for now. I had always been interested in the logistics of crime scenes,

The Disturbed

and maybe that was why the murders that happened in the back here were so much a part of my thoughts. But there was the aspect too of my wanting to make peace with the whole incident having to live here now. I knew where I wanted to go in life, and I guess that was why I could not stop smiling, I was finally on my way.

I finished what I had to do just in time as Lacy pulled up in the driveway. I went out to greet her.
"Hey baby!"
"Hi, how are you smiley?" she says as I grab her and squeeze her tight, planting a kiss on her lips so strong she almost could not get the words out.
"I'm terrific! How is the love of my life doing?"
"I'm terrific as well, and so happy to hear the great news babe."
"The interview was so down to earth and comfortable. Mr. Burn's is truly a genuinely nice guy, very family oriented as well. I am going to really enjoy working for him. He started me off pretty good with the pay too which made me extremely happy."
"Beautiful!" She kisses me again as we walk towards the front door of the house.
"Oh, and did I mention that dinner is ready? Are you hungry now?"
"Yes, I am, and ready to taste your cooking."

We sit down for a nice dinner and the sun starts to set. I pop the cork on the Champagne and talk about our day as we eat. That was another thing I loved about Lacy, I could listen to her talk forever and stare at her while she did. We sat down to watch a movie we both loved after dinner leaving the mess for the morning. A half hour into it she looks at me with those eyes. The "want eyes" and I knew just what it was she wanted. I was her desert. She kisses me passionately and doesn't stop. I press stop on the movie and pick her up carrying her to the bedroom laying her gently on the bed. I continue to kiss her as she starts to moan. I know she wants me back as I watch her squirm all over the bed. I start to unbutton her blouse and gently kiss her breasts, as her moans get louder. I move down to her belly, grabbing her hips tightly letting her know I'm going to give it to her.

I lift her up, sliding myself gently inside her as I back her up against the wall. She moans loud, and her purr like noises making me thrust deeper inside. She claws my back as she bites my bottom lip; her way of saying I want more! Just then she whispers in my ear, "Give me all of you baby." I thrust deeper inside her as she moans louder "Auh! Auh! Auh!" I grab her ass by the handful, and squeeze it tightly, kissing her hard....I fuck her hard until I am about to cum then take her to the bed gently laying her down as I kiss her neck. I move down to her

The Disturbed

breasts sucking them as I squeeze them firmly in my hands, they fill my hands perfectly. The mirrored headboard of my bed shows her squirming as I move around her body down to her precious treasure, which is as tasty as a fucking ripe peach. I kiss, and lick her belly teasing her for a moment, moving to her sweetness. I grab her clit with my mouth as my lips, and tongue pull her into my mouth, she fucking moans loud, so loud I know Jazz must hear us in the other room. I suck her harder while I slide two of my fingers deep inside her, "Oh God!" she screams wanting more. I give her more tickling her with the tip of my tongue, going in and out of her with my fingers. I suck her until she cums in my face licking up every drop of it. I start moving slowly back up her body kissing, licking, every inch of her. I look up at her giving her a look of dominance, claiming her as mine. I suck her beautiful breasts again leaving my mark just underneath, kissing, licking, and gently biting her neck I thrust deep inside her giving her all of me like she asked for, her back arches, and she screams with ecstasy. She grabs my ass pulling me inside her deeper, "Fuck babe, take all of me!" and that she does. I thrust as deep as I can go looking into the mirror as I do and I am all of a sudden shocked, I can't fucking move! Not sure what to do or how to react to what I see in the reflection of the mirror. I am worried what Lacy will do if I freak the fuck out but it's too late I am past that! I jump up in a fucking panic grabbing a sheet to cover her as I run to the window. The sliding glass doors are full of the mist from the fog of the night, but that was not what freaked me out. On the outside of the glass doors was written "I can see you!" I yell to Lacy to get dressed as she looks at me with fear in her eyes.

"Is everything alright?" she asks as she walks over to the sliding back doors. Her mouth drops open.

"No babe, everything is not alright. I don't know what to do about this either."

"Should we call the police?"

"I am not sure they will do anything about a peeping-tom? I am wondering how long they were watching us, and who the hell it is. I mean why would they be walking around in the back of the woods like this? I sure the hell wouldn't."

"You have a point there, especially after what had happened not too far from here, unless they don't know about that?"

I throw my clothes on and run out of the room calling for Jazz. I knocked on his door but there's no answer. I slowly open the door and notice he's not even home. What the hell? I thought he was just here an hour ago and he didn't ask to use my car or anything.

"Lacy, I am going to take a quick look around outside okay babe. I will be right back."

The Disturbed

"Derek, please don't be gone long, I don't want you out there alone and I don't want to be in here alone either. I mean what if someone is out there babe?"

"I just want to take a quick look real fast and I'll be right back here with you." I tell her as I kiss her on the forehead and run out the front-door. I am not feeling too good right now, my stomach is in knots, but I could not just sit there. I wondered if it was the faceless fuck again, I wondered if he knew where I lived. I took a quick look around and saw nothing at all. No one, but it was pretty dark, all I had was a fucking flashlight. All of a sudden, I hear something I turn around and see Jazz coming up the driveway.

"Hey Jazz, where the hell you been man?"

"I came out to get some fresh air and the mail at the box man. Why what the hell's going on?"

"Lacy and I were in my room and I noticed someone had written "I can see you" on my fucking back-door man."

"Wow! What the fuck? Did you find anyone out here?"

"No man, but yeah that's what the fuck I thought, who the fuck would be out here so fucking late peeping in fuckin windows, God damn perves."

I walked back in the house and see the look of shock on Lacy's face, my walking in the house with Jazz. I knew what she thought and had to clear that up fast.

131

"Jazz was out for a short walk and checking the mail box, but he said he didn't see anything either. I will keep a better eye out around here and definitely put some drapes up covering the back-door. I am sure it would not hurt to make sure all the locks here are solid."

I take Lacy back to my room so I could talk to her about the things I should have told her a while back. We sit down on the bed still a bit edgy from what had happened.

"Lacy, there is something I need to share with you although I am not sure if this is the right time to bring it up, but I don't really think there is a right time to bring it up."

"Okay babe, I'm all ears, what's up?"

"You know when I met you I told you that I go to therapy right?"

"Yes, babe and I think it's a good thing that you go."

"Well, I never really told you why I go and the main reason why I moved here from the city. What I am trying to say is sometimes I see things that are not there, but to me they are very real. In fact, so real I have been almost wondering if I am really seeing them or not. I know you know I have battled depression and stuff and take medication to sleep, but the medications also help with alleviating the delusions as well. I was not keeping it from you I just didn't want you to be scared of me without first knowing who I really was inside."

"Babe, I do not look at you any different now that you have told me. I love you and know who you are inside

The Disturbed

and I love the entire man that you are. I don't love you because you are perfect or don't have flaws, I have some too. My love will never change nor will the way I view you. We can manage this together if I can help in anyway."

"You are one amazing woman and I thank God for you Lacy. I have to share with you that there is this one thing that keeps happening to me, and the problem is I am not sure if it is a damn delusion or someone actually stalking me. There is this man who has been following me around for about two years now. I call him the "faceless fuck" only because I don't know what else to call him or it... "it" has no face. He has a head, but as far as facial features there are only indents on his face, talk about fucking freaky. This is one of the reasons why I have had so many issues in the past with sleep. It's also the reason why I moved to Alabama. I felt if I got away from the city maybe my mind would somehow react to my surroundings more normally. But to tell you the truth Lacy, I have seen the faceless fuck here too and on the way here as well. It's been so hard for me to deal with alone. The hardest part is I really wanted to know if I am crazy or if what I am seeing is real. It feels real to me even though I can't explain that to a tee. My therapist says I am doing much better here and overall my stress level has gone down a great deal so that tells me I made the right decision coming to live here, and after meeting you well, I am convinced there is no other place for me.

"Lacy, I can't help but wonder if that faceless fuck wrote that because one night I saw him at work on my night shift at the gas station a little over a week ago. I don't think he would know where I live though. Remember the night I called you pretty late? That was the night I saw him. I didn't want to freak you out that night, but you sure helped me stay calm when I was freaking out myself."

"So, do you see him follow you?"

"No, for the most part just appears out of nowhere freaks me the fuck out, smirks at me, and then leaves. He has never said anything to me, but I'm not even sure if "he", "it" can even speak with no open mouth area, I mean it could be a mask. I have never really seen him up-close. It sure has tormented me for years though." It was hard to sleep that night. Lacy fell asleep in my arms but I kept waking up looking around and listening for any type of movement. I was still worried if it could be him or not and my anxiety was out of control. This guy not only invaded where I came from he had invaded where I was at....but why? I had never had any real enemies that I could think of so none of it made sense except I was a loon, and it was in fact the fucking dreaded delusions. I mean apart from the writing on the backdoor slider there was no proof anything was real, and who knows who did that, could have been anyone.

I wrestled in my mind about it for hours until I guess I passed out. I woke up in the same place with Lacy still in my arms and the TV still on. My plan today was to

The Disturbed

make sure the house had some really good locks, so we felt a bit more secure. I also planned on adding some motion-lights all around the house to help keep peepers away, if that's what it was anyway. It was Friday, so I have to train Jazz at the gas station tonight and the next two days, then my days there were done. Oh, I could not wait. Lacy and I had to make sure we registered for our classes on Monday, but thank God, we still have two weeks until school starts up again. I wanted to feel comfortable with my new job before I start my new classes. It seemed everything was coming together despite the fear that was unsettling about the peeping-tom incident.

We got to registering for classes and managed to get two together, which was nice. I loved seeing her smile throughout the day even for a short time, yeah, I had it bad, the love bug that is, and there was no stopping it now. We made some breakfast together which to me was so romantic. I know a man saying how romantic it was to cook with his girl, how masculine right? But it was the truth; I loved doing even small things with her. Love struck for sure. Jazz had just left for his first job at the grocery store. He had been working there about a month now and seemed to like it. I felt pretty good about him taking over the gas station now because I saw how well he was holding up at his current job, I was actually pretty proud of him. We had known each other so long I could not hold a grudge long about my car loaning incident. Lacy and I sat down after breakfast and watched a movie before it was time to go our separate ways. She liked old movies just like I did, in fact there were a lot of things she liked that I liked as well such as fishing, although we hadn't gone together yet. We got cleaned up and it was time to say our goodbyes for the evening and I walked her to her car. I hated when she had to leave or I had to leave her. Even though it was always for a short while, it seemed like days, and time passed so slow without her near me. I miss her deeply and I could tell our relationship was getting more serious for her too. I noticed she always felt really at home when she was over now.

Five o'clock came around and it was time to head to the dreaded gas station again, but at least Jazz would be with me so I was not as freaked out thinking about the next additional two days of training over the weekend.

"Hey Jazz, man it's time to head out. You ready?"

"Yeah man, coming, just let me grab a jacket."

"No prob, I'll be in the car."

"Okay!"

We get to the gas station and I decide to let Jazz do most of the work tonight, seeing that he will be taking over in two days. He didn't mind. But of course, it was a quiet night, not many customers at all.

The Disturbed

"So, what happened last night man, I mean with the writing on the slider and all? I mean what were you guys doing, getting it on or something? Did you see anyone or did you get a look at them or whoever wrote on the glass door?"

"Well, to be honest we were very involved and heated, and no I didn't get a look at the guy. I wish I did. I ended up telling Lacy about my delusions though, which was very hard. I have still been having them even living here although they have not been as bad. I was worried what she was going to think of me. She sure is special man."

"Yeah, I can see that. It must have been hard telling her about the delusions though, maybe you need new meds or something man? I know I have never seen you so involved with a girl since I've known you. How did she take it?"

"Her being the amazing girl that she is, she took it very well. She loves me for me and that is what I have always longed for in a girl. She's not just beautiful outside but so much more beautiful inside as well. I think I will marry her one day Jazz. I really do."

"Awesome, well good luck to you guys. You make a great couple."

"Thanks man, of course if I ever got married you would have to be my best man. I mean who else could ever fit that spot but you? We've been friends since we were kids man, and I think this move was the best thing we could have done."

"Yeah, I agree, my life is starting to take shape. Thanks for the thought too of best man, that's sweet." Jazz says laughingly, which I found to be rude but maybe he was just being jealous again. I laugh it off too.

"Don't worry man you will meet someone soon. You never know. I sure didn't drive here thinking about meeting a girl. Then met the best girl I could have ever met."

The night seemed to just drag on. Finally, it was time to close up. I let Jazz do that as well and coached him along the way. He did a pretty good job with everything and had remembered everything I had showed him before. I knew he had this in the bag. Working here would be no problem for Jazz at all.

We got through the weekend without incident and Jazz was ready to take over the gas station on Monday. I, on the other hand, was getting ready to start my own new job, and school again. It had its pros and cons for sure. I mean although I was taking this new job on and changing my hours because I wanted to also spend more time with Lacy it looked like it would be a while before we could actually do that. At least we had that to look forward to, and our time apart would sure make being together exceptionally special.

Jazz was working two jobs now and hardly home; I would see him from time to time but only coming and going mostly. He had been working the grocery store for a couple of months now, and the gas station for two

The Disturbed

weeks, and doing a pretty damn good job at it from what I heard. He had saved up some money and asked if I could take him to look at some cars.

"Hey Derek, will you be really busy next weekend?"

"Just hanging around the house with Lacy for a while taking a break from the week is all probably. Why? What's up man?"

"I wanted to know if you could take me to look at a car I had my eye on? I know you have been helping me out with rides and I have the bus, but I really think it's time for me to get a car, and I have been putting money away after I pay rent and stuff to be able to get a car and I think I have enough cash now."

"Nice man! Yeah, sure we can go do that, I want to get a new fridge for the house as well. We have really grown out of this small one here in the house. I can get that done that same day. You think you can help me load and unload the new fridge while we're out? I may have to rent a truck for an hour to take it home. It will have to be Sunday though; I have to work a couple of overtime hours on Saturday."

"Sweet! Oh yeah man, no problem. I have to work on Saturday as well, but Sunday is perfect. I don't work until the night shift at the gas station on Sunday though. Oh, hey I didn't tell you, but I met a girl at work when I was working the register. That's kind of another reason why I need to get a car soon. She gave me her number, but I want to be ready to be able to take her out ya know."

"Nice man! I told you your time was coming. She was around here somewhere you just hadn't bumped into her yet. Good luck with that Jazz. So, have you called her or planned a date or anything yet?"

"Nah, man, I was trying to think of how I can ask her out without a car and not have her look down on me, but I don't want to put her off for very long and have her think I am not interested, ya know?"

"Sure, that makes a lot of sense to me man. Okay, look just talk to her on the phone and be honest with her. Tell her you just moved here, you work two jobs, and are going to look at a car this weekend and would love to take her out after you get one. Then you guys talk about what she likes and where she would want to go. Believe me honesty is the best policy."

"Yeah, you're right Derek, I think that is the best way to go about it too man. "Thanks. I appreciate the help, all of it, I really do. It will be a way for her and I to get to know each other a bit before we even go out, if she is okay with moving that slow."

"Only one way to find out; talk to her man, don't be shy, go get her."

"I will call her when I get home, thanks again Derek. Talk later, got to get to work."

"I hear ya. I am off to do the same, late Jazz."

The Disturbed

"Late man." Jazz yells as I hear the screen door slam shut from him running out the door. It was looking like both of our lives were heading in the most amazing directions and all we did was take a chance and move into the unknown. I was so glad we did.

CHAPTER 7

Call for Back-up

Monday came and it was time to start my new job, well my training anyway. I was so excited about it I didn't sleep much the night before. I pull up and walk into the office and asked them if they could let Mr. Burns know I was here for my training. Mr. Burns comes out to greet me as he did before and introduces me to Pete.

"Good morning Derek."

"Good morning Mr. Burns." I shake his hand firmly.

"Derek, this here is Pete, he will be training you for three days. After that you should be able to take on the route alone. I have faith in you Derek, you will do just fine."

"Thank you, Mr. Burns, I am very glad to be here and can't wait to get started."

"Well, alright then, I will let you two get going. Pete will show you all there is to know. If you have any questions feel free to ask him, he has been here over ten years."

"Sounds good! Mr. Burns, thank you." I shook his hand, before we head out the door to get in the delivery truck we will be taking. We started out the route right away and boy did I start to understand fast how much this was going to work my body out. Pete, showed me my whole route and what I would be doing. Oftentimes, the clients were not home so you have keys to let yourself into the properties to deliver. I didn't mind, I was used to having the whole job on my shoulders and the responsibility of someone else's place so to speak. I would have approximately nine barns and ranches to deliver to each day. Before I knew it I was on my own working my own route and loving it. Some days I would get up to eleven a day depending on how big the loads were that the clients ordered. Part of the duties on the job was to load the trucks with the hay bundles, it wasn't fun but I did enjoy the fact that I was also getting a nice workout and Lacy was starting to enjoy the results of my toned body as well. Let's just say it was working out for the both of us in the romantic area.

I delivered to some very nice ranch homes and would find myself day-dreaming about the kind of house I wanted

The Disturbed

for Lacy and me. It was nice meeting so many of the polite customers who quickly became friends. Alabama was very different than Cali. I mean folks just loved each other right from the get go here, and there seemed to be no second guessing anyone here, at least where I lived and delivered to. It was like we were almost family at least treated as such. I would be unloading the hay bundles then a customer would offer me lemonade. When I told Mr. Burns I was not sure how to handle it, he just said,

"Oh, that son is normal around these parts, especially from the clients of mine who I have delivered to for over twenty years. Just give a big smile, and say thank you." He said, that was all I had to do. I thought to myself I sure like it here.

Three weeks had passed and it was time to now add my classes to my already full schedule. Lacy was pretty busy as well but we were still managing to see each other on our days off and she spent the night a lot more which made things around the house so much more comfortable. Jazz had asked me about two weeks ago if I could take him to go look at a car he was interested in. However, I was called in that Sunday to work another shift so I had to cancel on him. Today was Sunday and both of our schedules worked out to have today off so I could take him to look at the car and finally get that new fridge we had needed in here. Jazz had been talking

Shawna Mccallister

to the girl he met on the job at the grocery store for a couple of weeks now and she had also seen him at work a couple of times he said. I think he was a bit pissed at me because I could not keep my word to take him two weeks ago, but I have to do what I have to do. I mean work has to come first especially it being a new job. I go tap on Jazz's door to see if he's up:

"Hey Jazz, you up? Did you want to still go look at that car today?"

"Yeah, hey, give me about a half hour and I will be ready to go. Is that alright?"

"Okay, no problem I'll get something to eat while I wait. Let me know when you're ready."

"Okay."

That was weird. Jazz didn't sound like himself. He almost sounded depressed or something. I hope he wasn't pissed at me still or anything like that. It wasn't like I just made other plans on purpose; I mean I had no choice to do what I had to do. Maybe he had been working too much? I know how that is when you get on overload; it was probably the fact I had to flake on him the last two weeks too. I kiss Lacy goodbye while telling her in her ear I would see her when she got home. It was cute because my house was slowly becoming her home and I think we both enjoyed that feeling a lot. It wasn't something we had talked about it was more of something that just seemed natural

The Disturbed

and happened on its own. That's another thing I loved about Lacy and I, nothing ever felt pushed, rushed, or fake. It was always on the real, completely solid. We had no insecurities with each other, at least that I knew of, of course I had my own insecurities about myself, but the way she made me feel eradicated them all.

I made a bagel with some cream cheese, had some coffee while I waited for Jazz to get ready, and I found a place to get a fridge after we were done with the car run. I also sat there and reflected on what the officers had said to me that night they came to the door a couple of months ago, asking if we had seen anything suspicious about the area. Then I thought about the sliding glass door incident and it bothered me even more. I had done all I could do personally to secure the house as far as the motion lighting and locks, I also had the gun my dad had given me as a going away gift. He gave it to me privately as to not alarm Mom or any of the others. Hell, Jazz didn't even know I had it but I was sure glad I did. Dad and I went to the range a lot when I was a kid, well into my teenage years, so I felt very comfortable using one and my aim was dead on. Dad had taught me well in this area too, and when we would go on fishing trips without Mom we would have fun setting up our own target practice of course using dummy bullets. I didn't want to tell Lacy about the gun in the house either because I didn't want her being all paranoid about it, so I left things the way they were, peaceful.

"Hey Derek, you still here man?" I hear Jazz yell from the other room.
"Yeah man, I am waiting on ya. You ready?"
"Yeah, I am coming, just let me get my shoes on and I'll be right out."
"Okay, ready when you are."

He finally emerges from his room ready to roll. We head out the door on our mission.
"You got the address for the car man?"
"Yeah, it's not too far from here, on Kenworth Street about five miles away I am thinking." I put it in the MapQuest and Jazz was right about five miles away.
"So, what kind of car?"
"It's a '63 Nova; the owner said it's in really good condition inside and out. I guess the kids Dad owned it, and the Dad passed away, and for some reason the kids were really having trouble keeping it around."
"I mean I can understand that I guess, if it's bringing back sad memories or hurtful ones sometimes it's better to just move on you know."
"The guy who now owns the car says he had three other cars and this is the one he decided to sell. I was actually surprised he still had it. I thought someone would have jumped on that by now, but maybe it's meant for me. I am sure if it was for sale in Cali it would have been bought already for sure."

"I have to agree with you on that one."

"If I like it, and buy it I plan on really fixing it up, making it into a chick magnet you know."

"What do you mean chick magnet? What happen to you and the girl you were talking to?"

"Oh, her name was Kimberly, I guess she got tired of waiting around for me to get a car? She does not answer her phone anymore when I call and I have left a few messages, but none have been returned."

"Oh, crap man, I'm sorry. I guess some of that is my fault not being able to take you to get the car sooner. I really am sorry man. If it was not a new job I could have taken off, but there was no way for me getting out of that when I have my word for overtime when I took the job."

"I get it man, no worries, if she was meant to be in my life maybe she would be but she's not, so fuck it. Time to move on, right?" Jazz turns to me and gives me a deep stare. I can tell he's pissed and resentful, but maybe he's also hurt, and feels rejected too. I felt really bad even though there was nothing I could do. But his stare was almost frightening.

We arrive at the man's house who is selling the Nova and the car is outside. From the looks of it the man who owned it, who had passed, sure took care of it. It was in great shape. Jazz goes up to the door and knocks.

"Hello, Is Tim here? I called about the Nova, my name is Jazz."

"Yes, hey, I'm Tim. Nice to meet ya Jazz. There she is, feel free to take a look inside while I go get the keys."

"Great! Thanks Tim." Jazz opens the driver's side door and takes a seat.

"Nice! I can't wait to hear what it sounds like." The interior was so clean my mouth dropped open. For once I was jealous of Jazz. Well, not exactly, extremely happy for him, but I loved this car. The guy Tim we had just met came out with the keys and Jazz fired it up and boy did it sound good too. Again, my mouth dropped and I thought to myself they sure don't have deals like this back home. Jazz's face lit up. I could tell he was taking this car home, I had known him enough years to know how he thinks by now. He revved it up a few times and got under the hood to take a look as well. It was even clean under the hood. I was starting to think to myself, "Okay, what's the catch here?" But there was none, here was just a nice guy who wanted to let go of some memories that seemed to hold him down. I guess he was ready to part with it. After all the inspections of the car Jazz started talking money.

"So, how much will you let her go for?"

"Well, she's pretty clean. I was thinking about five-thousand dollars. "You know what, I am not even going to talk you down for this car, you got it, man. She's a beauty and well taken care of I can see, well worth all five G's."

"Thank ya much, let me get the paperwork and you can take her home."

"Sounds good!" Jazz counted out five-grand for the car and I sat there thinking how it was a miracle this car was not sold already, but I guess it was meant for Jazz. Might I just add what a deal, Jazz practically stole this amazing ass car from this guy and to tell you the truth I would not have argued the price either. Jazz got all the paperwork squared away with Tim; they exchanged the money and shook hands.

"Tim, thank you for sure, a beauty car, I will take good care of it my friend."

"I appreciate it Jazz, I am sure she will treat you good. Take care now."

I got in my car and Jazz got in his. I pulled up alongside of him.

"Hey, did you still want to go with me to get that fridge?"

"Sure, let's go man, I am cruising now." We both laugh out loud.

"Okay, follow me; let's get us a new fridge." I knew it was not as exciting as the new car Jazz had just gotten but I was excited about the fridge because we had been using that small one for months, almost a year and it was time to up-grade, and well it was going to be new. I felt I needed something new now.

We get to a Home Department Store, and find a nice fridge for a pretty good price. I had to rent one of the trucks from the store to get it home, but at least it would be there today, another plus side was I had Jazz to help me load and unload it as well. I figured I would leave my car there, then Jazz could follow me home help me unload than I would take the truck back. The day seemed to be working like clockwork, it's like the damn stars were all aligned or something. The fridge ended up being heavier than we thought but we man handled it and got it in the house. I got ready to take the truck back as I got an eyeball full of Jazz making love to his new car; well it was new to him anyway. I waved as I passed him, he barely looked up, but who could blame him, I would be doing the same damn thing with that car. The guy sure got a deal.

It was getting late and I decided to cook some dinner before Lacy got home. She had gone shopping with her Mom all day, which was good because I know she needs her own space away from me as well. I guess I do too but for some reason all I want to do is be with her. I mean I get it when she does things without me, but most of the time I just sit and wait for her unless I am not studying. Alabama is so much of a slower state than Cali, but it wasn't just that, it was the fact that this woman had

The Disturbed

my heart, mind, and complete attention, which I could not ever see changing, especially if it depended on me.

Monday came fast and not only was it a long work day, but it was time to start our night classes. I was tired but I was pushing to get there. I finally got to the school, glancing over, I see Lacy looking as beautiful as always, saving me a seat right next to her. I was glad that school was finally starting up again now because Lacy and I had so much fun in class acting like teenagers. It reminded me of how we met and how our relationship developed; I think it did her as well. It was something we shared together that kept us young, for some reason I think we both found it sexy as well. I mean, I would be sleeping with the girl who sat next to me in class who I had this extreme crush on. Of course, she was pretty much considered mine but the fantasies we shared sure made it hot in the bedroom. That's one thing that was so hot about our relationship; we thought alike about mostly everything. Passing sexy love notes back and forth about what we wanted to do to each other later was hot. Of course, we couldn't act on them in the class, but we sure fantasized about them during class. She made it so hard to focus but I loved it, I felt alive and never wanted that to go away.

"Hey babe, I'll be right back okay, going to the restroom. Want a snack or anything while I'm out?"

"No hon, I am okay…thank you."

"Okay."

Shawna Mccallister

I stand as quietly as possible and make my way to the exit door of the classroom. The hall was empty and quiet. I get to the restroom, which has been newly remodeled and I'm impressed. I do my business, walk to the sink looking around at the new décor that had been upgraded. The restrooms had patterns on the walls of blue diamond shaped tiles, but what I like the most was the mirrors. They were set on a rod-iron frame, looked like something I would have in my house, sure didn't look like a college bathroom mirror. There were a few feet between the door and the sinks, now and the restroom had a long entrance. I washed my hands, looked up to check my handsome self out, make sure my hair was in place, then I saw him! He was right behind me! He wasn't close because of how the bathroom had been changed. I stood there in panic mode, and could not move. I tried to look at him as long as possible to get as much information about him as I could. What the hell was he doing here? What the fuck did this guy want with me? Was he even fucking really there or was I fucking seeing shit again? All of these questions ran through my head within seconds. He stood there as if to block the door with that smirk on his face same as I had seen all the times before. This time I was scared. I mean, did he want to kill me? What the fuck did he want from me? I don't look away, I can't, I have to know what the hell is going on with this shit, so I glare back. He makes a move

The Disturbed

as if to come forward to me and I fucking freak the fuck out. I take my eyes off him for a second to see what I could use to help me fight this guy off and look back up. He is fucking gone! I don't know what the hell I feel right now. Was I relieved? Did I want to finally beat the shit out of this guy so he would quit fucking with me? All I know is without thinking, I started for the door to see if I could see him anywhere. The entrance was right there and I knew he used it. "Fuck!" another instructor heard me yell loudly as it echoed down the college build halls.

"Are you okay?" They asked with a tone of concern.
"Oh, yes sorry, I'm okay. I just had an issue but I resolved it. I apologize for the inappropriate outburst. I know classes are in session right now." Her eyes still gazing at me with concern.
"Okay, well I am glad you've gotten everything resolved. Please try and keep it down out here as you said classes are in session now."
"Yes, ma'am, I will. Thank you."
"Thank you." She turns and walks away.

I know Lacy is wondering what the hell happened to me by now and I am so rattled I don't even want to go back to class but next to her is where I feel the very best. She calms me just my being beside her. I slowly walk back to my seat and sit down. Lacy gives me a look of concern as I look into her eyes she knows something is not right with me. Class lets out and she rushes me to the halls to talk to me.

"What the hell happened to you?"
"Lacy, I saw him here."
"Who here? That guy who has been following you?"
"Yes, he was in the bathrooms here and I got really freaked out because I was alone and there was like no way out of there man. He looked like he was coming toward me but when I looked away to see where I was going and looked back he was fucking gone. What the hell is wrong with me Lac?"
"Maybe there is someone following you babe? I think you should call your therapist and make an appointment though hon. I mean just to talk it over and see what she thinks."
"Yeah, I think you are right…you are always right, I am so glad you love me like you do Lac. I have the best girlfriend on the damn planet."
"Come on, let's go home babe and get some ice cream and cuddle…sound good?"
"Sounds perfect to me." I kiss her on the forehead, and hold her close as we walk to the cars. She follows me home and that's what we did all night, eat and cuddle.

This next weekend was the Harvest County Country Fair in Wellington and we all planned on going. At least I knew

The Disturbed

Lacy and I were going. I was kind of excited because I had never been to a real country fair before so I was ready to try some chili and have some fun, take my mind off work and school for a while. Both Lacy and I had the night off from school but we did have to study so I decided to make a run to the store for some coffee for us. It had been a long day and Lacy decided to stay and wait for me. Jazz was home so I didn't really mind much I felt she would be safe and the store was only about five miles away. I give Lacy a kiss and head out the door for the coffee.

"Hey Lacy, where is Derek going?"

"Oh, hey Jazz, he's going to get some coffee. Did you need him?"

"Oh no, I was just thinking maybe you and I could fool around."

"What did you just say?"

"I was just kidding man, don't have to get your panties in a wad."

"I don't play around like that Jazz, not even jokingly, okay?"

"Okay, okay, damn...sorry. So, how did it feel knowing someone was watching you guys that night when you found the writing on the back door?"

"Not too freakin good! Jazz have you been drinking? Because you are really asking inappropriate questions right now even for you."

"Even for me? What the hell does that mean?"

157

"What I mean is that you are normally not like this with me Jazz."

"Well, we are normally not alone, are we?"

"Wow! Can you tell Derek I am studying in the room when he gets back please?"

"Nope, I am sure he will find you pretty pants."

"You're a sicko."

"Thank you!"

Back with the coffee I walk in the house and find Lacy in my room with the door closed, which I find kind of weird. I open the door and she's sitting on the bed with her class books open.

"What's wrong honey? I thought you would be in the other room studying, was Jazz being too loud or something?"

"No, babe I actually got freaked out by Jazz. He was not acting the normal way he does, staying to himself. He was flirting with me and calling me pretty pants, shit like that. So, I came in here because I felt uncomfortable being around him."

"Are you serious? Now that pisses me off! I'm going to have a fucking talk with him and if that does not stop he's out of here. I will not tolerate anyone treating you with disrespect especially in my house. I'm sorry babe." I kiss her gently on the forehead.

"Hon, don't start any trouble, I am sure he's probably having a really bad day or something. It was just weird is all, not like him."

"I am going to talk to him about it and you let me know if it happens again okay."

"Okay."

I really felt this time Lacy didn't trust Jazz, and I was not about to leave her alone with him again. Her telling me there is something offish about him, and he seemed to be flirting with her was too much for me to hear. I left it alone only because she had asked me to, but I sure had problems getting it out of my head.

The Wellington Country Fair

It was the third week of October, and every year Wellington put on this big Country Fair for our city. I was kind of excited to take Lacy, not only so she could show me around, but so I could taste all the chili's that were made for the contest, Oh, and there was also a pie eating contest, which I was surely interested in entering. The fair was more like a carnival, there would be rides and cotton candy, stuff like that and I sure needed a break, so did Lacy. It was getting dark which is the best time to go I hear from Lacy because the whole place lights up, and it gets really festive. We were ready to go so I stepped in to ask Jazz if he was going to go with us to the fair and he said he planned on staying in for the night. I guess he said he was catching something from work and wanted to rest so he wouldn't miss any work, which made sense to me. So, it was just me and Lacy and I was glad. I wanted to be alone with her anyway under the moon and stars.

We arrive at the fair and it is lit up like Christmas. There were a lot of booths which included the chili booth where we were able to taste all types of chili and slip a note in a box for the voting. As well as the amazing pie booth where they had just about every pie you could imagine, which I might add was Lacy's favorite part of the fair. But then there were the rides. We have a bit to eat so decided to place some of the carnival games while our food settled. Of course, Lacy beat me in every game except for the ball throwing games where I won her a stuffed scarecrow, which thank God had a smile on it. Not that we were in any competition or anything but she enjoys the competitive side of playing. That's probably why we wrestled so well together and ended up making love, we both had it in us and it brought us closer together. After a few carnival games we decided to get on the ferris-wheel because it was one of the slower rides to start out with after having eaten chili. We are high above the city overlooking the lights of the carnival and all I could think about was this would be a good place to ask her to marry me someday. Although, this wouldn't be the night I sure had a clear fantasy about it which I planned on making a reality next year. While on that ferris-wheel at that moment I found myself hoping that she would say yes to me even a year from now. The ferris-wheel came to a slow and we are at the top for a few minutes and she leans against me hugging my arm tightly. I look into her eyes, and we both start to say I love you at the same time. I gently kiss her lips as the ride starts to move again. Another beautiful moment I will never forget. The ride moves us down to the bottom where we can get off; both excited to go get on a faster ride. We start to run to the rollercoaster which is about two rides away playing the cat and mouse game which was really cute. Lacy loved for me to chase her, tickle her, and of course wrestle with her all the time. I loved the tomboy in her.

"Derek, I forgot my scarecrow on the ferris-wheel!"

"Okay, I will run back and get it, stay here at the rollercoaster in line for us okay."

"Okay, hurry, I hope no one took it, it is special to me." I kiss her on the forehead quickly and race off to retrieve the scarecrow. The ferris-wheel is in the back of the carnival so not much of a crowd back there but a few who want to ride of course. I approach the ride operator.

"Hey there, did you happen to find a scarecrow on any of the seats of this ride we just got off of?"

"Yep, sure did. Here you go."

"Oh my God, thank you so much, it's very special to my girlfriend."

"No problem, have fun."

"Thanks again!"

I look down at the scarecrow thinking how glad I am that we found it and how odd it is for me to care so much for a stuffed doll, but it was Lacy who made that stuffed doll come alive. I looked back at the man who had found it for me and smile. Then I see him, in the background of the ferris-wheel. I think real fast if I had taken my meds today and I had. What the fuck was going on here? God damn not here too! He gives me a smirk's smile and starts to walk towards me. I drop the scarecrow, and realize it picking it back up fast as I start running back to where I left Lacy. I reach her and my breathing is out of control, my anxiety is at full extreme right now. I try and talk but I have to catch my breath.

"He's here! He's fucking here!"

"Who's here Derek?"

"That faceless fuck I told you about who I also saw in the school bathroom. What the fuck is going on?"

"Babe, try and relax okay. We are okay right now that's all that matters. You are with me and we are safe." Lacy tries to calm me. It works on the surface

The Disturbed

but I am a mess on the inside wondering what is happening to me and why? I try and focus on getting on another ride but I can't stop looking around for him. I am worried for Lacy as well. What does this guy want? I start to think it was him who wrote on my bedroom backdoor. I just have a gut feeling and I am worried because he saw my Lacy. My mind is racing and I can't slow it. Lacy looks at me and knows there is no calming me.

"Hey babe, how about we go home after this ride okay and watch a movie together and cuddle? I would rather be alone with you anyway sexy man."

"Really? That sounds wonderful...are you sure hon?"

"Yes, I am completely sure." She says kissing me sensually on my lips. Oh yes, she knows how to get my mind off of my troubles for sure and I can't wait to be alone with her now too. Man, this woman was magical, and knew just what I needed all of the time, even when I didn't know what the hell I needed.

"Hope we can handle this ride after the chili babe, this one is a lot faster."

"I am ready for it, my hearts already beating fast, so bring it on." She laughs at me and kisses me again. Boy was I distracted now. I wanted to get on this ride fast, get done fast, and get home fast.

"Okay babe, here we go! Hold on to your scarecrow this time will ya?"

"I will, I promise."

We get off the ride laughing our asses off because we didn't expect it to be that fast. Lacy still had her scarecrow and I was much calmer about being at the carnival than I was before the ride, but none the less ready to get home with my girl. We decided to grab some chili and pie to go for the movie at home. I felt bad wanting to leave so early, missing the pie eating contest and the chili cook-off results, but Lacy didn't seem to mind at all. We were so much alike and I loved that about her. She always made me feel like I was home in my heart.

There were so many beautiful properties I would deliver to. Most of them were ranch style homes with lots of acreage. I would always find myself day dreaming and sometimes even saying a little prayer about the future I wanted and hoped for with Lacy. Every stinkin home seemed to bring it out of me too no matter how old the ranch home was I felt the pull of the universe telling me that my destiny was with Lacy. There was this one I delivered to that was a two-story ranch style home and the wood it was made out of was to die for. I mean it was beautiful, the whole house was made of beautiful oak wood. I would just stand there sometimes with my mouth hanging open. I would think to myself this is what

The Disturbed

I want for Lacy and me. This was my goal, my motivation for delivering all of this hay every day and then going to school, this is what kept me going and dreaming. I guess you can say it was my mental vision board and I would soak it all up every time I took a break or even drove by. I thanked God for my job and often for what was happening in my life and for moving here. To this day I still believe it was the best decision I had ever made.

I arrived at the Crawly Ranch and got out opening the gate wide enough for the large truck I am driving, man do they have a beautiful place. The front gate entrance opens to the length which is about a foot from touching this long row of corn stalks, that seem to go on for at least a mile, but it's a beautiful site. You can tell these people take pride in their place for sure. I pull the truck up next to the barn after the long driveway of growing corn. I think to myself how glad I am that I moved here and how peaceful my job is, hard somedays but the surroundings really don't get better than this. I start to unload the hay which takes me about an hour because this customer wants things done a certain way. All the hay has to be put inside the barn and stacked perfectly. I don't mind, it's just a bit of a pain in the ass to get it inside the barn using the small dolly I have with the truck. But I get it done one by one. I am about done and I hear a car or truck near the gate area. I start to wonder if the customers had come home early and if my truck would be in their way. All of a sudden, I don't hear the engine anymore? Hum, maybe there is another house around here that I don't know about? I didn't remember seeing any other roads, but I wasn't looking for another road either. I have about another half hour before I am finished here, and I am getting tired. I sit in the truck to take a break, turn on the radio for a few just to catch my breath for a minute. All is calm than I hear a thump in the back, on my truck, I turn down the music and turn around but I don't see anything. Thinking nothing of it, I turn the music back up, and then I hear it again but this time it's louder.

What the hell man? I get out of the truck and walk around it, but I don't see anything. There is no dog or anything roaming what the hell could do that, I think to myself.

"Ppsssst!" I turn to see who did that.

"Oh, fuck!" Was all I could get out before I fall to the ground from a blow to the head, blood running down my face into my eye. I am panicked wondering what the fuck just happened. I nearly pass out, but as soon as I am able to shake it off I am hit again hard. What the hell? Does someone think I am trespassing on this property or what? Was all I could think and for some reason I wanted Lacy. I see more blood coming out of my head

The Disturbed

and I start to freak the fuck out. Is someone trying to fucking kill me or fucking what? I wipe the blood from my eyes with my sleeve so I can see just in time to miss a third blow aimed for my head; he was coming straight for me again with full force. I don't know how I did it, but I moved my head so fast the metal pipe missed me and hit the truck. I was going in and out of consciousness, I could barely see from so much blood coming from the first gash in my eyes but I wanted to know who it was that was attacking me so I managed to stay awake. I felt it was my life if I passed out. Finally, I see him, it's the faceless fuck! This fucker is really trying to kill me I think to myself as I try to gather my thoughts on how I can protect myself. I move to the inside of the truck so I could at least slide across the seats to avoid him. He smashed the windshield in sending glass flying everywhere, while he keeps hitting it, I grab my phone trying to dial 911, as another blow lands on the windshield again. I knew it was time for me to get out of the truck because he was determined to come in after me. I open the door and run to the back of the truck which is close to the entrance to the barn where I had been bringing in the hay. I turn around to check where he is, he's still in the front of the truck with that smirk on his face I had always seen. It fucking hits me, this faceless fuck is real. I am not having delusions it's been real all along. I leave the phone on the 911 call as I figure out what to do next, there was no time to talk to an operator, this was my life I was fighting for now.

"What the fuck do you want from me man? Why are you doing this?" I scream at him. He does not reply at all just stares at me with that same eerie smirk. He hits the truck really hard as if he wishes it was my head again. I'm scared but try to stay calm, I want to see Lacy again. I'm losing a lot of blood but try to stay focused on what's in the barn I can use to protect myself. I have never really been in any fights so to hit someone else was not my nature, but this guy was a fucking psycho and I knew it was either him or me. I remember seeing a fire extinguisher hanging on the wall and I knew how to use one because of my training at the gas station. I run in and grab it, while I am looking around for something sharp. I see a pitchfork on the wall next to where I had stacked the hay. I grab it and wait. He comes in after me and I spray him trying to get back out of the barn with the hay-pick in hand to have more room. I did not want to die in this barn or on this day for that matter, not like this, it wasn't happening. I was happy now, and no one was going to take that away for me, especially this faceless fuck. On the way out of the barn I see a gas can, I grab it hoping there is some gas in it, and there is. I take it with me. I set it down as he comes at me with the pipe again aiming for my head. I swing the pitchfork at him hoping to do some damage and it flies

The Disturbed

out of my hands getting caught in the pipe coming for my head. "Oh fuck!" I grab the gas, and open the can as fast as I can, and hop inside the back of the truck. I get close enough to gas him because I was able to hide it behind me as I move out of the barn. He yells. "Shit!" I am trying to think if I have ever heard that voice before, but I can't fucking think of anything except how to set this fucker on fire. Then I remember the truck window was rolled down when I was taking a break. I hop inside, and push in the truck cigarette lighter, this has to fucking work, I think to myself. I see him coming at me again he swings at me through the open window, and tries to get the door open. I grab the lighter, and hop out of the truck into the back again just in time. I know he's drenched in gasoline, and I pray this fucking hot car-lighter sets him ablaze, lights his ass up. I toss it on him as I jump from the truck knowing it may all go up. Sure as shit, the fucker ignites, and he is yelling. I am running not knowing what the fuck to do, and scared as hell. I have never hurt anyone or ever thought about killing someone, but this was self-defense for sure. He runs to the driveway, and I look quick to make sure he is still burning, and not coming for me. Trying to catch my fucking breath from what has just happened to me. I sit on the ground leaning up against a tractor to rest, and check my head. I fucking couldn't believe what the hell just happened to me. I am dizzy from the blows to the head, and do not even know how I managed to think as quickly as I had. As I watched him burn barely able to look, I had flashbacks of the last few years that this faceless fuck had been following me. I wondered if it was not all in my head, I mean was I really fucking having delusions or was this shit all real. A real fuck face trying to make me believe I was fucking crazy. The barn caught on fire the same time as I hear the sirens coming in the distance. I am not sure if they heard all that happened from the 911 call or not but I was glad someone was on their way. I sure needed help. I see sheriff's roll in first and then fire engine, they start to extinguish.

The town sheriff's see me and immediately order me to get on the ground. I put my face on the ground, hands laid all the way out. I tried to tell them this was in self-defense and that this man had been following me for years had just tried to kill me. After going through my wallet for my license and any other information on me, they put me in handcuffs and pull me aside for questioning.

"Son, what's your name?"

"Derek Holson sir"

"What happened here?"

"Someone tried to kill me sir, and I had no choice, I had to do all I could to protect myself. He hit me two times in the head. I was afraid for my life sir."

"Is that why you are bleeding?"

"Yes, the first blow to my head came from the back and I couldn't figure out why anyone would want to hit me like that or at all. I almost blacked out, but somehow, I stayed awake and saw it was the same man who has been following me for a couple of years now. You can confirm all this with my therapist. I have been going to one for a while because of this."

"Okay, wait here while I run your license."

"Yes sir." I sit there waiting nervously and wishing I had Lacy next to me or my Mom. God, I sure wanted to be home at that moment. A second officer came over and asked me about the incident and all that had happened all over again. I guess they wanted to make sure I had my story straight. I mean I did just kill a man, although it was all in self-defense.

They looked at me like I was full of shit, as if I was actually delusional. They sit me in the back of the police car while they check me out on their radio. I can hear them talking about what they see and what they thought about me. I heard one officer say:

"But there is no body. We can't just keep him unless the owners of the property press charges if there is no body, we have to cite him, and let him go after the property owners are contacted and arrive. I mean it's really up to them if they want to press charges or not. But we may want to put him on a psych-hold because he did cause harm to an individual's property and obviously to himself."

I'm fucking thinking to myself there is no fucking body? Not that I am excited that there would be, but what the fuck, someone just tried to kill me, and there is no fucking body! I lean my head back against the seat trying to make sense of anything that just happened, and can't. I mean I saw him burn, I poured that gasoline on him, I heard him scream. If there was no body and I am telling them I just killed someone they are going to lock me in a fucking psych-ward, especially after me telling them I have a therapist. Then I thought about Lacy, I thought about my job, I thought about my life, my Mom and Dad and how much I wish they were here right now. I needed them bad, real fucking badly; I wanted to run home, in fact in my mind I was running home. What was Lacy going to think of me? What was I going to tell my new employer? I loved my new job and my life. What the fuck was going to make all this go away now?

The owner of the property showed up and I have a chance to tell my side of the story. None-the-less they do not want me near their property again.

"Son, we hear what you are saying, but we would not feel safe leaving our property open to you personally again after what has happened here. I understand you were in fear for your life, but there is no evidence to prove this, and we have to make sure our livestock, and barn stays safe. We hope you understand where we are coming from. We do not want to press any charges against you, but we do suggest you get some counseling

The Disturbed

or help from your family to work all this out. We will do the clean up here, don't worry about it."
"I would like to pay for the cleanup at least, please."
"Son, I think you have been through enough, we will take over from here." I'm still in handcuffs and I don't think I will be going home tonight.

CHAPTER 8

Delusion or Truth

They put me in the back of the police car until the ambulance arrives to take me to the hospital for x-rays. I am feeling so lost right now, so fucking lost I feel crazy. Maybe I need a psych-ward, whether I need one or not I have a feeling I am going to be on lockdown. I mean, look at me, and look at what happened, there is no fucking proof I am a God damn sane person at all. I am sitting in the back of the patrol car just waiting to see what they are going to do with me. The officer finally comes to the door and opens it to talk to me.

"Hey Derek, how you are feeling?"

"Well sir, not to sound like an ass, but how do you think I am feeling? I do not understand what the hell just happened here, but again I'm certain someone tried to kill me. Now why, I don't freakin know, but I am feeling a bit unstable right now and would love to make a couple of phone calls."

"Okay, we are going to have the paramedics look at your head and you may have to go get an x-ray down at the hospital is that okay with you?"

"Yeah sure, I just need to make some calls please. Can I use my cell phone while you stand here?"

"Son, you are not under arrest, we are just looking out for your welfare right now and want to make sure you are okay to be by yourself. Yes, I think it would be a good idea for you to phone a family member or friend right now and have them meet you at the hospital. Okay?"

"Yeah sure, thanks. It would seem we want the same things right now. Sorry I am a bit pissed off at this whole thing because this was all in self-defense but I have no proof of that at all. What about cameras? Are there any cameras here at all that may have caught what happened to me and why I had to do what I did?"

"We asked the owners about the cameras, they said they weren't working, but a gentleman was scheduled to come work on them tomorrow, sorry son."

The Disturbed

"Oh, that's just perfect! Okay I will just make my calls and we can head to the hospital." I call Lacy first because I was so glad I was alive to even be able to call her.

"Lacy?"

"Hey babe, what's up?"

"I need you, can you come to the hospital near our house?"

"Why? I mean are you okay? Yes, I can honey. What's going on Derek?" I can hear panic in her voice.

"I had an incident with that faceless fuck that's been following me. Lacy he tried to kill me, but when the police got here they found no body and I sound crazier than I have ever sounded before in my life. But I was hit on the head twice very hard so they want to take some x-rays to make sure I am okay. I just really need you right now babe."

"I will be right there hon. I am leaving now, okay. Stay calm Derek we will get through this okay babe. See you in a few minutes at the hospital, okay."

"Okay, I love you Lacy."

"I love you too Derek. Everything's going to be okay." I get off the phone with Lacy and think about calling Mom, but I realize I would have to calm her down more than anything, so I decided to wait until later to call Mom. Her not being close to me would make her a nervous wreck and I didn't want to do that to her. I knew it was my reasonability to call my boss and let him know what had happened, that I was hurt and would not be able to return to work for a couple of days. I got the answering machine and left a brief message about what had happened and that the owners didn't feel safe with me delivering to them again, but that what had happened was not my fault. I would need a couple of days to heal and I would call when I got out of the hospital. I thanked him in advance for his understanding and hung up the phone.

The paramedics ask me a few more questions as they clean my head up from the blood that had run down my face. They bandage me up than put me in the back of the ambulance. We arrive at the hospital and I see Lacy pacing back and forth as they open up the back of the ambulance. The paramedics pull me out of the ambulance; Lacy sees me and comes running to me.

"Oh my God Derek! What the hell happened? Are you okay?"

"Yeah babe, I am okay and it's a long story, I will tell you everything as soon as they get done checking me out okay. I am so freakin glad to see you. Oh my God I have been through hell in the last three hours, and I do not know what I am going to do now."

The Disturbed

I'm not a crier, but as I look into her eyes a lost helpless feeling comes over me and I need her like never before now. I realize this woman is definitely in my life for a reason. After all, she has been the only one who I have been able to tell everything to and she still loves me just as I am. I sure need her to trust and believe me now like never before too. I mean what if she sides with the Sheriff's because there was no body. I mean clearly, she will know I am not the type to whack myself on the head a couple of times for blood and sympathy. I know she knows how much I love my job, which I may not fucking have any more either. My thoughts are racing and I can't slow them.

The doctor orders an x-ray which comes back normal apart from a concussion. They gave me something for my anxiety which was completely out of control. As I lay in that hospital bed praying that Lacy would believe every word of what had happened to me, much to my amazement she did. Of course, that is the type of woman and friend she has always been to me since I met her. She seemed very concerned though and suggested I take a couple of days to be evaluated. I know it was hard for her to be honest about that with me, but I agreed with her. I knew someone had done this to me, but I also needed a reason to take a couple of days off and maybe try a different medication, at least an anxiety medication now so I didn't lose it completely.

The hospital called my psychiatrist and with the remediation of the Sheriff's department as well I was willingly held on a 5150. That meant I would not see Lacy for at least seventy-two hours. I also did not want her to stay at my house during that time, I just didn't feel she was safe there, so I told her to go home until I got out and that I would call her from inside if I could. I didn't want much, just my fucking life back which seemed to have completely fallen apart in one hour. I made that dreaded phone call home to Mom and Dad. I hated to worry them but at the same time I needed them now really bad too. My life seemed so out of control and the fucked-up thing about it was I didn't do a fucking thing to cause it. I wanted to be back home for some reason, I needed this to all stop, I sure had a lot of thinking to do in the next three days.

I tried to call Mom after I had gotten off the phone with Lacy, but I got her voice mail. This was not a situation where I would want to leave her a message but I knew I may not have another chance to call for a while, and I need to talk to her bad. I guess it's true that when we hurt the most we want our Mom, at least I felt this way right now. I needed some security in my life right now and Mom and Dad were the only security I had ever known. I scramble to know what to do when I hear, "Sorry we can't come to the phone right now" but I feel I have to leave a message.

The Disturbed

"Beep,"

"Hello Mom, Dad, its Derek. Umm well I don't want you to panic but I need to talk to you about something very important. I am not sure when I can try to call again because I will be in the hospital for a couple of days. Nothing is life threatening, but I just went through the worst experience of my life and I just need you. So, I will call as soon as I can okay. Please try not to worry and keep your phone on. I love you, talk soon." As I hang up the phone I swallow a deep feeling of being lost, as if I were a kid alone in a department store or something. I need to be home so bad, but I also needed Lacy.

While I was waiting I gave Jazz a call to let him know I would not be home for a couple of days. He was asking a bunch of questions as to why I was not coming home, but I was in no frame of mind to talk to him about what I had gone through. I was tired, drained, and beat-up. Lacy and I waited at the hospital for a couple of hours before I was taken to the lockdown, which I could tell upon arrival, wasn't a pleasant place at all. I was sure going to miss Lacy, but I also wanted to show her I was really trying to sort things out. Still I had no answers to what happened that day no matter how many times I went over it in my head, I would come up with the same thoughts. I don't know. I hated to admit it, but I didn't think I would be going back to that job I love so much,

181

nor did I think Mr. Burns wanted me back being such a liability to his company and all. I mean I was a new employee no matter how much I loved the job.

During my stay in the psych hospital I was kept on the same medication; however, they did raise it a bit. I was able to talk to a couple of different doctors in there, but I felt like this was not going to help me at all. I know what happened and I know what I saw. I know I am not as crazy as I feel right now, but there is no proof that I'm not, which makes me feel even more fucking crazy. Oh God, how am I ever going to make this right? I mean this shit is on my record now and I wanted to be a police officer. Yeah right, they will laugh me out the fucking door. My thoughts are racing as I continue to make sense of these last two days. This is the second day in the psych hospital, and I realize the only one that is there for me is me, and well Lacy. I start to wonder what Lacy thinks about me, does she think I am a fucking lunatic under that beautiful caring smile? What will I do if I lose her too? I can't bear to think about that anymore feeling as if any minute something is going to push me over the edge. Just then the doctor comes in and I ask him if there is anything I can take to help me calm down? I can't stop thinking about what happened to me, and replaying it over and over in my head. The doctor said yes, "I can prescribe you a low dose of something to help you calm down."

"Looks like you will be going home tomorrow. I understand you believe someone truly attacked you?"
"Yes, I know someone attacked me, I just do not have the proof that someone did."
"Have you filed a police report with the police department or sheriff's office?"
"Well, I told them what happened and it seemed as if they just didn't believe me because I have a disorder."
"I would advise you to make a report whether they believe you or not and do what you have to do to protect yourself. Make sure you give them a full description of the person who did this to you as best you can so you cover your own self when things like this happen."

I sure appreciated this doctor, for once I felt as if someone besides Lacy was hearing me, listening to me about this even being real. I mean he had to believe me a bit in order to be telling me to make a police report. I was glad to hear I was being let out to go home tomorrow, I just wasn't sure what to do with my life when I got out of here.

"Excuse me Doc, can I have couple of calls out to my parents please?"

"Sure, I will tell the front desk to let you use the phone to call out."

"Thank you, and thank you for listening to me, you are greatly appreciated sir."

"That's what I am here for Derek, glad I can help in some way."

I sit on the edge of the bed nervously tapping my foot on the stepping stool below my feet waiting for someone to walk in to tell me I can make a call. Finally, after about 10 minutes which seemed like a year someone comes in to tell me I can use the phone. It's a pay phone so I have to call collect which makes me feel unmanly but I am not in a position to worry too much on that seeing how unstable I truly feel inside. I decided to try and call my parents first because that is why I asked to use the phone and this is the first time I had gotten to try and call them back after having left that message. I dial and the phone rings, I am feeling nervous because I went from being the son they were proud of to feeling like a fucking misfit who almost wishes he never had to make this call, but would not be able to handle it being completely alone in this state.

"Hello?"

"Hey Mom, its Derek, sorry I could not call you sooner."

The Disturbed

"Oh my God Derek, what in the heck is going on there?" Mom was a complete mess, but I figured she would be after hearing my last message.

"Mom don't panic, but I am in a psych hospital. I was attacked at one of the residences on the job, and I had no way to prove I was, and they are not too keen on believing me on it because of my history of delusions. To tell you the truth the only one who believes me is Lacy, the girl I told you about, and one of the doctors here who seems to think I may be telling him the truth. He told me to make a full police report anyway. I mean they took a report, but I didn't make a report and give a description of someone trying to kill me yet because I was in shock that there was no body found."

"No body, Derek what the hell are you talking about?" Mom said in a stern voice, and she never said hell, ever.

"Mom, someone has been following me for a couple of years, I remember I had mentioned that to you and Dad, but didn't really go into much detail. I always wanted you and Dad to think the best about me. Well, anyway, this person for some reason followed me to Alabama, and tried to kill me. I was defending myself and set him on fire, but when they went to look for a body after all this happened there was no body Mom. I had blood gushing out of my head from the harsh blows he gave to me with a pipe. After this happened I decided to admit myself into a psych hospital for seventy-two hours so I could get some help understanding what the hell happened to me and to see if my medication was causing any delusions. I am going home tomorrow, and all they have done here was raise my meds a bit. At least one of the doctors here said I should make a personal report against the person who attacked me, but the problem with that is I don't know who it is. I have been a mess Mom, and I swear if it wasn't for Lacy I don't know what I would do. She has really helped me stay calm through this even though I still can't make any sense of any of it."

"What are you going to do when you get out of the hospital tomorrow, son?"

"You know Mom, I had not even gotten that far yet in my thinking. I just found out I could go home tomorrow a few minutes ago, so I don't know."

"Derek, you know you are always welcome to come home anytime. Maybe you should stay here a while until you figure what you want to do son."

"I will have to talk to Lacy about possibly going back there, we are pretty serious and I can't imagine my life without her."

"Well if she is that important to you son, she is more than welcome to come with you if you both decide that's what you feel is the best thing to do."

"Thank you Mom, I really appreciate that. I'm not even sure how she would feel about me leaving, let alone her having to leave all she's ever known to be with me. I sure feel like I need to be home for a while to sort this out and make sure I'm safe from this guy whoever the hell he is. Sorry Mom, I'm just a bit frustrated that someone can follow me around, come almost kill me and get away, while my whole life is ruined. I really loved my job Mom and this was not my fault. I guess that is the main reason why I decided to admit myself here because I have been so angry and in shock about the whole incident that I can't even sleep well lately."

"That is completely understandable Derek, you have been violated and traumatized and there is no one physically you can blame. That's hard son, I can't even imagine what I would do having had gone through something like that. I'm so glad you are safe and I want you to stay safe. You have to start at least using your camera if you see this person ever again to try and get some type of evidence so he can be caught. I also agree that making a report of this person and your own description of them as well as what happened is a good idea. But I am sure your father would want you to come home for a while as well, in fact I am sure of it."

"Yeah, I know Mom. I will give it some thought, I really will, I think it's where I need to be right now too. Well, I will let you go, okay. I will talk it over with Lacy, and see what we come up with, and keep you posted on any changes."

"Okay Derek, we love you son. Call us again soon, alright? I will tell your father what has happened and he may call you himself."

"That's fine Mom but please tell him to try not to worry too much, okay. I need to lay low for now and take one day at a time."

"Sounds good son, I'm proud of you and sorry this has happened to you, I know you were doing so well and were so very happy. You will get your life back son, like you said one day at a time."

The next morning, I'm let out of the hospital and Lacy comes to get me. I'm so glad to see her and never want to let her out of my sight again. It felt like we had not seen each other in a year. She was concerned and I could see it on her face. I get in the car and we drive back home to my house to talk and figure out what the next step in my life should be.

"You know Lac, I sure missed you while I was in there. I have been worried about Mr. Burns maybe not wanting me back to work for him."

"Yeah, I have been thinking about that too Derek, I don't know hon, all you can do is call and see if he will meet with you to talk about what happened."

"Yeah, I know, I was going to do that after I get home, get cleaned up, and love on you a bit, I mean if

The Disturbed

you want." I say to her as I give her those puppy dog eyes with a pout.

"I think I can squeeze you in, but I think you should at least make a call to see if you can get an appointment to see Mr. Burns first babe."

"You're right; I will do that first, then take my woman."

We get to the house and it is a mess. The kitchen is full of dishes and the living-room looks like Jazz had been living in it the whole time. Lacy hangs out in my room while I take a quick shower before calling Mr. Burns. I just get out of the shower and I hear the front door close. I throw my robe on fast because I want to ask Jazz what the hell happened to the house. I come walking out of the bathroom and see Jazz.

"Hey Derek, how's everything going?"

"Not so good Jazz. What the hell happened here man, did you have a fucking party or what? I have never seen this place in such a fucking mess, I hope you know you are cleaning this shit, not me."

"Sorry Derek, I had an accident at work yesterday, and my hand and arm got burnt trying to put out a fire from a cigarette someone threw in the trash can next to the gas station. I was told not to soak the skin and to try and keep the skin dry, so I've just been keeping it wrapped and putting Aloe-Vera burn cream on it to soothe it, but I will get to it Derek."

"Oh, sorry to hear that man, didn't mean to jump on you like that, I've had a real fucked up week. And thanks, I would appreciate it being cleaned up some."

I head back to my room and want Lacy so bad, but I am so distracted and irritated by Jazz and the shit that has gone on. I ask her if we can spend the night together tonight so I can just try to save my job. She gently kisses me on the forehead and sits next to me. I can't help but kiss her, I missed her so much while I was in the hospital. I somehow control myself, get up from the bed and get dressed. I sit back down and take a deep breath while I reach for the phone to make the call I am so dreading to Mr. Burns. I dial the number and the phone rings.

"Good morning, 'Burns Hay' how may I help you?"

"Hello, good morning this is Derek Holson calling, would it be possible to speak with Mr. Burns please?"

"Sure, let me see if he is available please."

"Thank you." I wait on the phone nervous as hell wondering what's going to happen. I'm hoping he will understand, but I also know this is a big issue for the company. I hope he didn't lose the customer because of what happened. I'm still pissed off right now too because none of this was my fault either.

The Disturbed

"Hello, this is Mr. Burns how can I help you?"

"Hello Mr. Burns, it's Derek Holson calling. I wanted to know if you would have any time this afternoon or anytime really to meet with me so I can explain what had happen to me at the customer's farm where the fire was. It was not my fault and I truly am sorry for any problems I have caused being out of work due to the accident as well."

"Hello Derek, well it would seem we lost that customer's account, and they are also suing us for damages to their property."

"Mr. Burns I offered to pay for all and any damages that occurred on their property, which I also tried to explain to them were not my fault, but someone was trying to kill me."

"I'm sorry for what happened to you Derek, but son we have a business to run here and we don't need lawsuits coming at us. I'm going to have to let you go Derek. I know you are a good friend of Lacy's, but we are in a tough spot now and have to put the business first. I hope you understand and I wish you the very best son, I truly do. We have your final check here if you would like to pick it up."

"I understand Mr. Burns; I will be in to pick it up later this afternoon. Thank you for listening."

"Okay Derek, I will leave it with the receptionist for you, and do take care. Good luck to you and Lacy, Derek."

"Thank you, Mr. Burns."

I get off the phone and all I can do is hang my head in disbelief at what is and has happened to my life in the last week. I mean I even offered to pay for the damage and they didn't want me to, what the hell? I was sad, pissed, and discouraged to the max. I didn't want Lacy to leave my side. I lay on the bed and she laid her head on my chest.

"Babe, I just lost my job over this crap, and I was the one attacked. I'm a mess right now. I mean this shit was not my fault!" I yell as I feel tears welling up in my eyes. All I can think of is all the fucking dreams I had been thinking of through the months. Proposing to Lacy, buying a home, having kids with her, and now my fucking life has gone to shit because of a psycho fuck that I have no information on.

"Sorry babe, I don't mean to yell I'm just at a loss for words or answers for myself at this point."

"I completely understand Derek, I would be too hon. I don't blame you at all, I don't even know what I would do or feel having gone through all you have, but I am here for you babe, okay?" I squeeze her tightly and feel I never want to let go.

"Thank you for being here with me and loving me through all of this crap, I don't know what I would do without you." I wanted to bring up what my Mom had said but I didn't know if it was the right time or not, but at this point I figured when was the right time for anything? My whole life was changed within one week. Here goes...

"Lac, I spoke with my Mom yesterday and told her all that had happened to me. Well, to make a long story short she said I could move back home for a while until I feel ready to make some new plans or get back to work. She also said you could come with me, and well I wanted to ask you if you would consider coming with me if I moved back to California?"

"What about school and everything, hon?"

"I don't think I can go back right now, I just don't feel I'm ready. I mean losing my job really did a fucking number on me babe. I wish I could but I think I am done here. I feel like I need to be home for a while to heal mentally."

"So, are you saying you want to move back home for sure?"

"Well, I guess I am, and I'm hoping you will go with me. I can't imagine my life without you Lacy." Lacy looks me straight in the eyes as if the world had just stopped turning. My look back to her is intense as I wait for her reply. I can feel our emotions running through our stare. I know I need her with me, but love her enough to let her be where she would be most happy. We seem to speak words without saying any, our hearts connecting on a level that is beyond logic. It feels as though I am holding my breath waiting for her reply...

Shawna Mccallister

"Well Derek, there is no way I am going to stay here without you, you are my life now, and where you are is where I want to be. So, I guess if you are going to California, so am I." I grab her and throw her on the bed kissing her all over, and for the first time since the attack I felt relief from the hell I had been through during the last two weeks. She brought me back to life just like that; this woman is the one I will never let go of.

"What do you say we get some dinner then give Mom a call and tell her we are coming home?"
"Sounds good to me, let's get a movie while we are out...I think we both could use some comedy right now."
"You got it baby!" I feel alive, as if I have been reborn into a whole new life. I have to admit letting go of the old life I had planned for a while hurt, but I also had no choice. It's like the universe was in control now and well maybe that's how it needed to be. But, for whatever reason, I was finally okay with it. She was coming with me and she was all I really needed all along.

Lacy and I run out to get some Chinese food and a movie. I thought about all the things we would have to make ready in order to leave. I was also happy to be leaving this house; it just didn't feel like home anymore. Then there was the fact that I had to let Jazz know I would be

The Disturbed

moving back and see what he wanted to do, either stay or go with me, I mean it was the right thing to do considering he was my roommate and all. We go back from the dinner and movie run and Jazz was home. Good timing, I needed to tell him as soon as possible what I was planning so he could be ready either way.

"Hey Jazz, you got a minute man?"
"Sure, what's up?"
"Well, I wanted to let you know I am planning to move back home for a while. That incident really made a mess out of my life Jazz. I plan on taking Lacy with me. I just wanted to let you know to give you time to decide what you wanted to do as far as stay here at the house or go with."
"Oh, okay, thanks for the heads-up, work is going really well and having the two jobs I think I can take care of the rent here by myself, besides I kind of like it here. I wish you both all the luck in the world though, and hope you call once in a while."
"Okay man, that's understandable. I will call and check-up on you bro, you know that. How's your burn healing?"
"So far so good, thanks for asking. I just have to keep it clean, but it's almost healed all the way now."
"Good to hear, well we are staying in tonight for a movie."

"Nice. I have to work tonight so you guys will have the house all to yourselves."

"Okay Jazz, stay safe out there, no more playing with fire." I was surprised how I could make a joke like that after all I had been through, but I knew I had to start putting it past me somehow.

Lacy and I get done with dinner and decide to give Mom a call, feeling a little nervous I pick up the phone and dial.

"Hello."

"Hey Mom, its Derek, how is everything?"

"Derek, hi son, how am I doing? How are you doing son? I have been thinking about you a lot today."

"I'm good, well we are good. Lacy is really keeping me together. I think this is the one Mom." I say as I look Lacy straight in the eyes.

"Mom, I called to ask if the offer to come home is still open, and to bring Lacy with me, I really feel I need some time to get over this and home is the best place to do it."

"Of course, Derek, you are always welcome here at home son, and I told you Lacy is as well son, I know you feel strongly about her as well. Anyone who has cared for my son during his most trying days will always be welcome in my home. I'm sure your father would agree with me.

That was one reason why he married me." Mom giggles a bit, I felt not only to lighten the mood but she was elated that I was coming home. She sounded as if I called to relieve her from stress, not knowing before I called that that was indeed what I was doing.

"When did you guys plan on coming home?"

"Well, this week if that's okay with you and Dad."

"Of course, it is okay, it's more than okay."

"We have some errands to do here, then we'll load up and go, that's the plan so far."

"Great! I know your father will be happy to have his fishing buddy back, that's for sure. His buddy Hank is getting up there in age you know."

"Yeah, I'm sure he is by now. It will be great to go fishing with Dad again and show Lacy the cabin. I want us all to go next time, okay Mom?"

"Sounds good to me Derek. Well, you guys get everything together and get your butts down here. Let me know when about you will be here so I can cook you one of your favorite dishes okay?"

"Thanks Mom, you are amazing. I will let you know when we are on our way, and Lacy says thank you as well."

"You both are welcome, I love you Derek stay safe son and call if you need anything okay."

"I will Mom and thanks again you are the best Mom in the world."

"I have the best son in the world. Keep me posted. Have a good night, son."

"You too Mom, tell Dad I love him and I will see him soon."

"Will do, son."

"See you soon." I hang-up the phone and hug Lacy so tight. I felt alive again. It was so hard to believe how so much could happen in such a short amount of time. I went from having everything I was working for to losing it all and feeling like I'm on top of the world again. I couldn't wait to get home and for Lacy to meet my amazing parents. I only hoped it would not be too hard on her parents letting her go, but I knew it would be. That was next, talking to Lacy's parents. I was not looking forward to letting them know I was taking their daughter away from all she knew here and had going for her to be with me in California, I almost felt guilty but I also knew it was where she wanted to be as well.

We decided to go talk to her parents that night. I mean we were excited and planned on leaving as soon as possible so why wait? We drive up to her house and my heart is beating out of my chest wondering what they will say, wondering if they will talk her out of going with me, wondering if I am doing the right thing. I knew this was what we both wanted and I had to trust if it was meant to be then it would all work out. I took a deep breath as

The Disturbed

I closed the car door, met her on her side as we walked up to the house together.

"How are you feeling Lac?"

"I'm feeling great babe. Don't worry, everything will be alright"

"Okay, I believe you."

Walking in the door Lacy yells, "Mom, Dad?"

"We're in here Lacy."

"Hi Mom, Hi Dad, Derek is with me. We have something to tell you. I hope it will not be too much of a shock to you, but I am just going to come out and say it. I'm moving with Derek to California." Quietness fell over the room. I felt like running out of there it was so thick, but I knew I had to stay, and stand with my girl like she had done for me so many times before.

"Lacy, can we ask you why you are moving to California?"

"Well, Derek had an accident at work, and has had a hard time recovering, and said he was moving back to California, and well I love him, I can't imagine my life without him." What a woman, she just blurted out the truth like it wasn't shit and I'm standing there with my tail between my legs. But also knowing I was not in a position to stand-up to anyone really, I just wanted to find happiness again and I knew it was with Lacy.

"Lacy can we speak to you alone for a moment please?"

"Sure, Derek can you please wait for me in the living room?"

"Sure, take your time hon." I sit on the couch and my feet will not stop tapping the floor. Maybe they are telling her every reason why she should stay? I mean did I really have a right to take their daughter away? My thoughts raced through my mind non-stop. I sat there for about twenty minutes then she came around the corner. My eyes opened big as I waited to hear what she was going to tell me.

"Well, they don't like it but I am going anyway if that's okay?"

"Are you sure this is what you want babe?"

"I'm positive Derek; I will not live without you!" I pick her up, swinging her around in circles kissing her all over her face. This was really happening it was real; the girl I loved more than anything was not letting anything stop her from being with me. It was time to go home, I knew why I had come all this way, and it was to find my Lacy.

Lacy gave a short notice at work and we both canceled our classes that we had registered for in the fall. Then we took the next couple of days to decide what we were bringing with us. It wasn't hard really because we were alike in so many ways; we felt we only really needed each other. I mean we had our necessities such as clothes, computers, and special mementoes, but other than that we were starting over and we were okay with that. Lacy

The Disturbed

decided to leave any big things she wanted to keep with her parents and I didn't have anything big I wanted to keep but what I had bringing with us. We go rent a trailer to hitch to my car and instead of Jazz's stuff going in the back with mine its Lacy's, what an amazing feeling that was. We both agreed that it would be smart for her to follow me in her car because her car was new and we would need it back home, so that's what we did. We got a pair of radios to talk to each other the whole way which was so damn fun. It would cost a bit more to gas up two cars rather than one but, it would be so worth it later. I had been doing alright since the ordeal at the ranch that cost me my job. I've kind of just tried to put it out of my mind focusing on the excitement of starting a new life with Lacy in the place I had been raised. I could not wait to show her around California, I knew she would love it. What was even better is she was just as excited as I was to be going home with me. I couldn't say the same about her parents, but I knew we would be sure to visit or even maybe invite them to Cali sometime.

It was the end of the week, time to get on the road back home. We were ecstatic about leaving and I felt a closeness to Lacy I had never felt before in our relationship prior to now. Everything was packed and all we needed to do now was let Mom and Dad know we were on our way. After checking in with Mom it was time to eat some dinner get to bed and head out in the morning. Lacy and I lay in bed most of the night cuddling and talking about what it was like in California. We talk about our dreams, fears, plans, and how she was feeling about meeting my parents for the first time. Needless to say, we didn't get much sleep that night, but it was a night I was sure to remember.

CHAPTER 9

Going Home

We take the long trip back home with Lacy behind me all the way. I can't wait to give Mom a hug and introduce her to Lacy. Lacy is a lot like Mom, always putting others before herself, maybe that's one of the traits I noticed first about her other than her beauty. We drive up into the driveway, I see Mom and Dad coming out the door to greet us. I have never felt so happy to be home in all my life.

"Oh Derek!" Mom says with tears in her eyes wrapping her arms around me tightly with a big smile on her face. She gives me a bear hug like I have never had before, understanable considering I have never been gone this long.

"Hi Mom! Hi Dad! Man, I have missed you and this place so much. This is Lacy, the love of my life, and the one who has kept me going through the entire BS I have been through."

"Hello Lacy, it is so wonderful to meet you. I want you to feel right at home here, okay? Our home is your home and we are excited to have you with us."

"Thank you, Mr. and Mrs. Holson, I appreciate the warm welcome. Derek has told me so much about you both; I am excited to be here as well. It's interesting but I don't miss Alabama at all." Lacy says with a big grin.

"How about you both come inside and let me get you something to eat." That was Mom's favorite thing to do, make guests feel welcome with her food. I guess that was just her way of showing her deep love and appreciation for their presence. But boy was it a deep love that satisfied anyone's taste buds. Personally, I could not wait to get in the house and taste some of Mom's cooking again. I missed it and I could not wait for Lacy to taste what I was always bragging about for herself.

"Hey Dad, what have you been up to lately?"

Well, I'm retiring this year so I have been pretty much getting ready for your mother and I to have some get-a-ways. Nothing major just something the two of us have always wanted to do. I still have until the middle of next year so maybe we can all get down to the cabin for some fishing. I haven't gone since you and I went last Derek."

"Wow! Dad, that's been a while. How about we go to the cabin this weekend? I am sure up for some fishing and we could show Lacy around a bit too. I am sure Mom would like to get out of the house a while to."

"You know Derek that sounds like a plan to me. Let's do it. This weekend it is!"

"Yes!" I was excited to show Lacy the cabin and thought to myself it would be nice to someday take her there to be alone just her and I. But for now, I was happy to be with the family again after feeling so insignificant back in Alabama. Home was where my heart needed to be right now and I knew I made the right choice coming back here.

"So Lacy, is this your first time coming to California?"

"Yes ma'am, my very first time, and I can't wait to see all the things Derek has told me about. I really appreciate y'all having me here on such a short notice. I knew I could not stay back in Alabama without Derek."

"You are part of the family now girly." Mom smiles big as she sets a big plate of pancakes and eggs in front of Lacy. Lacy's eye open big and she turns to look at me with a big grin.

"Well, this is how it's done in these parts Lacy."

We eat until we can hardly move and I take Lacy up to my room to show her around.

"We have a guest room down stairs Mom said you could sleep in. It's just the way she and Dad believe. Waiting until you get married to sleep together, but I am sure they know we have. I think it's more of a respect of being under their roof thing, just for now okay." I kiss her on the forehead, thinking of how much I wish she was my wife already but I know it will happen soon. We sit on my bed and she opens up and asks:

"So, what's the plan babe? I mean what do you want to do while we are here, and have some time off?"

"Well, I think for a couple of days we can have some fun showing you around, and going to the cabin this weekend, but after that I plan to look for work, get back to my therapy, and pick-up where we left off in college. All we have to do for that is transfer our credits babe. I mean, you do want to stay for a while right?"

"Oh yes, sorry hon, I didn't mean for it to sound like that. I just wanted to know when I or we should start looking for work and maybe find our own place. I know that will take a while to get everything situated but I just wanted to know what was in that pea-brain of yours." She laughs, and I toss her back on my bed tickling her and kissing her on the neck.

"I plan on looking for work within two weeks, right after Thanksgiving babe. We do have a few thousand

The Disturbed

saved up between you and I so we will be fine. I have about twelve-thousand saved from living in Alabama, having low rent, and working so many hours, plus the school loan helped a lot keeping me ahead. And there are always places to be alone hon. I want to take at least that and get settled in therapy again and college for both of us, then get a good paying job so I can get us a decent place to live. Does that sound good?"

"That sounds perfect to me babe. Yeah, I have about the same, so I guess we will be fine money wise. I want to get to know your parents and spend time exploring Big Bear with you, and California. I love the warm weather, so far it's really nice, and sure is beautiful here Derek, makes me truly wonder why you would ever leave such a place." I look her deep in the eyes and tell her what's on my heart.

"Well, despite all that has happened that's been negative I know the main reason now why I even came to Alabama, it was to find you Lacy. I would have never guessed I would find someone so perfect for me so far away, but I did and I would do it all over again just to be with you."

"Come here you!" She kisses me on the lips and I see Mom out of the corner of my eye knock on the door.

"Hey Mom, we are just excited to be here."

"Well, keep that excitement zipped up until y'all get married, ya hear me."

"Yes ma'am," Both Lacy and I say back to Mom.

"I'm going to go shopping for some groceries for the house you both want to go with me and help me carry the stuff in?"

"Sure Mom, we can do that, as long as we can take a long nap when we get home."

"Deal! Now let's go, I'm not so young anymore and waiting on you two is making me older." We all laugh and head down the stairs. Mom always had a great sense of humor and I think that was one thing Dad loved about her, she had a way of keeping him going even when he was tired.

I love it here, and Thanksgiving is in about two weeks, so I knew why Mom wanted help at the store, it was a damn zoo.

The weekend comes and I am so freakin excited to get to the cabin and show Lacy around and make-out with her in the woods. Mom and Lacy are getting the lunches ready while Dad and I get the tackle, poles and all the gear we will need to catch us some dinner. I am feeling like a new man not having had any delusions since that incident at the ranch. I'm still taking my prescribed medications and plan on seeing Dr. Joanna Searian, who's the same therapist I saw before I left for Alabama. Once in a while I get down thinking about how much this was not my fault but then I look at Lacy and where we are, being home again and I can't help but think the universe had to be planning something beautiful despite all the hell

The Disturbed

I had been through. I sure had a wonderful woman by my side that I know the universe had a hand in picking for me; there was really no other way in explaining it. Unlike living back in Alabama, I wake up now with unexplainable gratefulness instead of a schedule in my head. Something has truly changed in me and I guess it took losing everything I was and had to gain everything I truly needed in life.

We get to the cabin and the day is perfect. We fished most of the day and caught dinner and then some. Lacy and I played around in the water for a while enough to get stinky, I'm sure glad the cabin has a shower because this water up-here is pretty fishin-nasty, but it was fun. Lacy and I went for a hike and made-out behind some trees. That was not all I wanted to do there but I had to try and be respectful of Mom and Dad at least. It had been a while since Lacy and I had slept together like we were used to and man did I want my woman. Then out of no-where, I hear Mom say, "Guys, come get some dinner!" it seems to radiate straight in our direction too as if she knew right where we were. I yell back "We're coming Mom!" We enjoyed a great dinner as a family then started a camp fire which was always my favorite part of coming here. There was something about it that made me just forget about the world and just be. Now Lacy, the love of my life, was with me, roasting marshmallows and making s'mores. Looking at the stars, there was nothing better than that moment, it was the only place I wanted to be and wish I would never have to leave. I think Lacy felt the same. Mom and Dad looked at us as if they remembered spending days like us together as they whispered to each other on the other side of the fire, Mom having that gleam in her eye as if she also knew that Lacy was the one for me. She knew I was gone, deep in love, and there was no return for me. As much as we tried to slow down and enjoy the weekend the faster it seemed to go. It was early evening Sunday and it was time to pack-up and head home. I could not wait until Lacy and I could come here alone. Not that I didn't enjoy all of here as a family because I did, it was beautiful. But there was something about this place I wanted to have with Lacy all alone, this was where I wanted to make our children and our own memories, at least that was what I dreamed about doing anyway.

This next week was full of calendar day appointments but at least we were getting shit done. I wanted to get therapy going, and Lacy to feel like she was moving forward too, so we planned on going to the college to register for Spring classes. It would be a wait but I would be looking for work this next week as well. I mean I was feeling good and Thanksgiving was just around the corner, I just really wanted to show Lacy I meant business, and I planned to make her happy and secure, as much as was in my power. Dad had told me that Home Deports

The Disturbed

Services was hiring and he had known a manager there for some time. I decided to give that a try.

Monday morning came around and we were off on our agendas. The nearest college to us was Crafton Hills College at a distance of about eighteen and half miles from center of Big Bear Lake. But it was a start and I'm sure it helped Lacy feel like she was accomplishing something at the same time. I mean we weren't in a hurry to graduate in the next year, but as long as we were working toward our goals it made us both feel more content inside. After registering for our Spring classes, I dropped Lacy off to spend time with Mom and I made an appointment with Dr. Searian for next Tuesday evening, then decided to go put in an application at that Home Deports Services Dad had told me about. Mr. Burns had told me he would give me a good reference because I was a good hard worker for him, not basing it on the incident that had happened but my work performance. I also had Sam too as a great reference and school so, I think with Dad knowing the manager I had a good shot at getting in there. I went to drop off Lacy after we were done at the college. Dad told me who to ask for and wished me luck. It was strange but I wasn't nervous at all, which I found odd for me. I was calm as if it was just supposed to be, as if everything was just supposed to be just as it was happening right now. I guess you can say I had a bit more confidence that the universe was on my side after all I had been through in the last two years.

I got to Home Deports Services, and asked for Tim Hawkins, that was the name Dad had given me and had said he was a longtime manager here.

"Yes, he's here may I ask your name please, I will let him know you are here."

"Yes, ma'am, my name is Derek Holson, I'm here to apply for the Wood Cutter and Power Tool area. May I please have an application while I wait?"

"You sure can, here you go. Mr. Hawkins will be right with you Mr. Holson."

"Thank you."

I sat there and filled out the application which was not that long at all. I was almost done when I heard my name being called.

"Derek Holson?"

"Yes sir, I am Derek Holson."

"Nice to meet you, I'm Mr. Hawkins, but you can call me Tim if you like."

"Great! Thank you, Tim. Nice to meet you."

"So, I have heard a lot of good things about you Derek, and don't worry, your Dad and I go way back. We knew each other during our war time. So, anyone

The Disturbed

he sends me has a job, especially his son. Not that I will go easy on you here, you will have to work your ass off, but as far as you wanting to work in the Wood Cutting and Power Tools department that my son is yours."

"Wow! I sure appreciate that and both what you and Dad have been through. This could not have come at a better time. What are my hours?"

"Well, you will have to work some Saturdays and off and on Sundays but I can start you at eleven dollars an hour just to start and I will give you an evaluation in three months for a two dollar raise, does that sound fair? Monday through Saturday with alternating Sundays. The hours will be from seven a.m. to six p.m. except for the Sundays you will be scheduled for will be seven a.m. to one p.m. How does that sound?"

"That sounds amazing to me, when can I start?"

"Let's get your application with all of your tax documents in our files, and you can start the day after Thanksgiving, so next Friday."

"Awesome!" I have the biggest grin on my face since I kissed Lacy for the first time, as I shake his hand with a hard grip wanting to show my gratefulness for giving me the position. I could not wait to get home and share the news with Lacy. I didn't want to just call her I wanted to look her in the eye and let her know we are going to have a great life here. It may take some time, but I had big plans for us and with the support of Mom and Dad I knew for sure we would be just fine.

When I got home I took Lacy to my room. I told Mom, Lacy and I had to talk and we would be down in a few minutes. Mom looked concerned but I wasn't worried, I mean she needed a little suspense in her life every now and then too. I sat Lacy down on the bed and looked her in the eyes.
"Lacy."
"Yes Derek?"
"Do you love me?"
"Yes, duh what kind of question is that?" She says with a big smile.
"I mean do you really love me?"
"Yes, Derek, you are scaring me what's wrong?"
"Oh, nothing but I GOT THE JOB!"
"Oh babe, that's amazing! I am so proud of you Derek. My gosh, that was fast, you were gone maybe an hour, if that?"
"Yeah, I know, Dad had a hand in it too but it's amazing like you said. I start in the Wood Cutting and Power Tools department the day after Thanksgiving. Monday through Saturday, with alternating Sundays. It pays eleven dollars an hour to start but in three months I get a two-dollar raise, eleven hours a day, I start at seven a.m. to six p.m. except for the Sundays when I will be

scheduled for seven a.m. to one p.m., shift, what do you think?"

"Sounds awesome babe, I am so excited for you and us. I am really loving it here and everything seems to be falling right into place ever since we got here."

"Yeah, I have noticed that too, babe. We sure have a lot to be thankful for don't we?"

"Yes, we sure do. I'm mostly thankful for you." I push her back on the bed kissing her and wanting her so bad knowing I can't take her because I want to respect Mom and Dad's rules. But soon we have to get away, just me and her before I just sneak her in my room. Hmm, I ponder the thought as I kissed her neck gently. Man do I want her and need her. Nothing like making love to the one you love after you get good news. Soon, Derek, soon, I think to myself as I pull her up, calm-down enough to take her back downstairs to tell Mom and Dad the good news.

"I really love you Lacy. You are my world and always will be. I want you to know that."

"I love you with all of my heart Derek. I truly believe we will be happy here together, I just feel it. This is just the beginning." My God her smile is so beautiful it lights up a room and when she says things like that it's sure hard to want to go down stairs. I grab her and say let's get out of here before we get in trouble. We both laugh as we rush down the stairs. We see Mom and she is wondering what's going on so I blurt it out, "I got the job."

"Oh, Derek that is wonderful." Mom says as she comes over and gives me a Mom bear hug. Dad, over in his recliner, looks over and our eyes meet as he gives me a thumbs-up. "Good job Derek." I think to myself, no pride here I am grateful my Dad loves me enough to help open a door for me right now. It was that time of the year too, where I was just really emotional with all the major holiday days just around the corner. I tried to soak it all in and let it become healing for me, I guess is how I felt.

It was Tuesday and time to check-in with Dr. Searian. I was a bit worried to go see her thinking she may not feel as much confidence in me as before I left. But I did have good news and I needed to probably talk about what had happened to me so she would understand how alone I felt in this not making any sense to me. I mean no one in the world could make any sense of this for me not even me who it happened to. But I knew when I was leaving there I had a lot of positive to share and focus on so I had to let all the other shit roll off of me, and that was the way I viewed it. My worst fears of the session were an illusion I had in my mind because she was glad to see me back and doing so well after such an event happening in my recent past. She was excited for me and Lacy and I left there knowing I had her full support just as I had when I left for Alabama. I thanked her, she gave me my prescription, and said I would see her in a couple of weeks. On the way home, I

The Disturbed

thought about how far I had come in such a short time, I truly felt the universe on my side, and miracles falling into my lap without effort and it felt good to be alive.

Thanksgiving came and as always Mom had the whole dinner with the works laid out for everyone and boy was I thankful. I was healing from the incident that happened back in Alabama, which made me almost lose my mind, now I felt like I was in heaven. Life can sure throw you some curve-balls, but some of them lead to beautiful places. Mom called us all to sit at the dining table and asked us to share something we were grateful for, which was pretty much a tradition in our home during Thanksgiving. We had a couple of relatives over that we rarely see, so it was nice to catch-up with them too. When it came to Lacy sharing what she was grateful for she said, "I am grateful for Derek and his beautiful family and being able to share this special day with you all." All I could do all night was stare at her and think about marrying her soon, in fact I was thinking about possibly asking her on Christmas Eve. She had no clue, but I had been pondering the idea for a couple of weeks, and now that I had a job, she was back in school in the Spring, and I had the money for the ring. It's not like we had to get married tomorrow, but I wanted her to be mine soon. I felt she was ready, and I really wanted her to be my wife. I hoped if she said yes, we could get married on

Valentine's Day of this year. I believed she was the one, and I didn't see any point in waiting unless she did.

Thanksgiving was beautiful, but it came and went fast. It was time to start my new job. I was glad that Mom would have Lacy here to keep her company at least until school started, I think Lacy likes it a lot too. I knew Lacy planned on going to work after school started back up but I was so glad her and Mom were bonding. I started work at seven a.m. on Friday morning. I wanted to learn everything there was to learn about the power tools in my section of the building and the different types of woods. Not only to impress my boss, but I wanted to fix stuff around my house when I got one soon and build things in my spare-time. Dad had taught me so much already, that's probably where I got the inspiration from. I realized just then that I had started dreaming about my future again, and God it felt good. I started to have visions in my head of what I wanted my life to be like, and feel like with Lacy, it felt like I was alive again in my heart. Being out of work for a while was taking a toll on me, but it didn't stop my enthusiasm about my new job or my new found hopes for the future. I felt deep inside this was the first day in many I would start to dream, and never look back to the hell I had been through. It was time to build my life and make it a reality for Lacy and I. I learned a lot my first day, but was dead tired when I got home. Mom had showed Lacy how to cook this roast-pie Mom makes, which is one of her famous recipes with the whole family. I was one happy man that night, work went well, dinner was amazing, and the woman I loved was sitting right next to me as I thought about when I would ask her to marry me.

It was Saturday, I was on my lunch break and decided to give Jazz a call and see what he was up to. He answers the phone on the first ring:

"Dude, were you sitting on the phone or what man, it barley rang." I say as I laugh out loud.

"Hey Derek, what's new man? How's the homestead?"

"All is well here man, how about you?"

"All is good man, just a little boredom here and there but nothing I can't handle. So, what's-up?"

"Well, Christmas is coming and I wanted to see if you wanted to come down man, I am planning on popping the question to Lacy on Christmas Eve. I was hoping you could be here ya know. I work a lot now but we can hang out too. I am sure I will get Christmas and Christmas Eve off; my Dad knows the supervisor."

"Wow, already huh, you guys ready for all that settling down stuff? I mean I know you love her but you think you been together long enough?"

"For sure. I have no doubt about her being my wife. So, what do you say can you get some time off to come down?"

"Well, I am not sure? When do you plan on getting married?"

"That part I won't know until I ask her Jazz, but I was hoping for this Valentine's Day."

"Oh, nice man! How about I plan to come down then? I know it's going to be Christmas and all but the store should be hella busy then and I know they will want me to work lots of hours. But I will plan to come down in February for sure would never miss your wedding if that's what you guys decide."

"Okay man, sounds good. Hope to see you in February then, hey I gotta go she's coming up the stairs. Late man!"

"Cool, let me know. Late!"

Lacy walks in the room:

"Hey hon, who was that?"

"Oh, that was Jazz, I thought I would give him a call to see if he wanted to come-down for Christmas, but he said the store really needs him during this time of the year. He did say he would come down soon though, which is cool."

"Oh, okay nice babe." She comes to lay down with me, lays her head on my shoulder and I kiss her on the head.

"I'm so glad you enjoyed dinner so much, I learned how to cook one of your favorite dishes today...yes!" She says with excitement.

"Thank you for thinking of me babe, I thought about you all day at work, I couldn't wait to get home to you. I miss this, our time cuddling and making love to you all over the house. I really want to move soon hon. I want to come home to your cooking and watch movies alone, take bubble baths together like we used to and just be naked with you." She laughs and kisses me on the lips.
"Derek, that's hot babe!"
"I know, and I want you bad!"
"I want you too, bad!"
"Well, we are going to have to do something about that soon before it gets too bad." We both smile, I kiss her, then hear Mom calling for dessert time. It's like she always knows or something, we both laugh, and head down stairs. Dessert then it's off to bed for the early rise for me.

I've been working for a few weeks now and I have really gotten to know my way around here and I'm pretty good about knowing all the major power tools in this place. I've actually had a blast cutting wood too, being able to use some of these amazing tools. I know which one I want for Christmas. Speaking of Christmas, it is two weeks away and thank God, my boss let me off after I told him what I had planned for Lacy and my family. It was time for me to punch-out on the clock and head home. I pass by Tim's office and give him a wave.

"Thanks again Tim for Christmas Eve and Christmas off, I truly appreciate it."
"No problem Derek, you're doing a great job here for us, son."
"Have a good night sir."
"See you tomorrow."
"Yes, sir."

I walk out to my car with a big grin on my face, get in my car and start it, thinking how I am loving life right now. I take a glance up and I freeze, I am paralyzed. I see that faceless fuck looking straight at me from the next row of cars in the parking lot. What the fuck is going on? I sit there unable to move as I stare at the smirk on his face again. What the fuck, I thought this was over? Oh, God help me. I call Lacy, but no one answers. I decide to just get the hell out of there and make sure he is not following me, but then I remember he knows where I live. My heart is racing, pounding out of my chest with anxiety. I can't seem to get home fast enough. I pull in the drive-way and run inside the house to make sure Lacy and Mom are okay.

"Derek, what's wrong? You look like you've seen a ghost." I look at Lacy, "I saw him Lacy, at my job, in the parking lot. I didn't know what to do, I freakin froze."
"You are sure it was the same guy Derek?"

The Disturbed

"Lacy, I am more than sure!" That was the first time I had ever raised my voice at Lacy, but I guess I was panicking bad.

"Babe it was the same guy, and I have seen him here before too, that's why I came home so quick to make sure you both were okay.

"What can we do babe?" I stare ahead with a blank look on my face as I realize there is nothing I can do, except protect my family as much as I can. Just then Dad pulls up in his truck, then walks inside the house to find us all nervous-wrecks knowing this guy, this man is now in my home town again. I try to explain as much as I can to Dad, telling him this was the guy who ruined my life back in Alabama, and tried to kill me.

"Well, Derek, looks like you have a stalker."

"Dad, this guy is more like a raging lunatic who seems to stop at nothing to make himself known to me, and I don't want another incident like what happened to happen again, ever. It shook me to my core Dad. That guy tried to kill me and has followed me back to California again."

"Derek, we are pretty protected here son with the alarm, cameras, and guns. I think anyone would be stupid to break-in here."

"I get that Dad, but this person has followed me around everywhere I go, and shows-up unexpectedly. I have to at least file another police report here in

California, just to be safe, in case he tries to hurt me again. Just to cover my own ass. I don't trust this asshole enough to throw him. Sorry Mom." I say as I put my hand over my mouth realizing my emotions have gotten the best of me at this point. I go hug Lacy, and tell her I am sorry for being short with her, that I was so worried for her and Mom. I thank God for her again that very moment.

CHAPTER 10

Heaven and Hell

Christmas Eve had finally gotten here, and I was excited. Lacy had no clue what I had planned for her today. I had not seen that faceless fuck since that last time in the parking lot where I work, but I thought about it every day, staying ready for him to show-up at any time. I tried not to let Lacy see this in me, the stress of it and all. Every time I would think about it I would just remember I was proposing to Lacy very soon, which kept me going through the last couple of weeks. It was a time to celebrate and I was not going to let this detour me from my plans, nor take the joy out of this season. It was a tradition to hand out one present on Christmas Eve, and open the rest of them Christmas morning. Mom always made a huge breakfast on Christmas morning. I was planning on proposing to Lacy with that one gift from me on Christmas Eve, which was the moment of truth I felt in my heart. Christmas Eve evening rolled around, we had all just finished an amazing dinner Mom and Lacy had prepared. We had a couple other family members over that we rarely see except for the main holidays like Christmas. We had all been drinking a bit of wine and champagne, which I was thankful for due to the fact that my life was about to take a drastic turn in one direction or another depending on what her answer was going to be. I took a deep breath and sat down next to the tree where all the presents were. Everyone probably thought I took a deep breath because I was full from all the good food we just ate, but it was my nerves for sure. I hand everyone one present and wait to give Lacy hers until everyone has one to open. I told Lacy that everyone would open their present one at a time so we could all see what each other got, it was more family orientated that way. She whispered to me "I agree Derek, great idea." So, I made her wait until last, as I sat there thinking how I was going to do this or what I would say. Mom snapped pictures while everyone opened their gifts one at a time. Then Mom says out loud, "Derek, where is Lacy's gift from us or you? Give her one, she should have been first being our special guest."

"I got it right here Mom." I reach way back behind the tree for a small box I had hidden so no one would find it. I pull it out, I look her straight in the eyes and all I could get out was "Lacy, I love you." I started to shake because I knew I still had to ask her the question. I take another deep breath and go to hand her the box but still holding on to it, I get on one knee. I could hear "Ohhh," from all over the room as if everyone knew, especially Mom. I take an even deeper breath, and open the box in front of her while we both have our hands on it. "Lacy, you have stood by me through everything, and have never questioned me or who I am even when I was not sure myself. You have been my rock and solid foundation when I felt my feet slipping. You have always believed in me even when I was not sure if I believed in myself, and I want to be with you, love you, and have a family with you only for the rest of my life, and even past that, will you please give me the honor of being your husband, and become my forever always wife?" The words just rolled out of me without thought, as if God himself had written them for me. Tears are running down her cheeks, so much so all she can get out real fast was a quick nod of, "Yes," then she throws her arms around me, and saying "Yes" loud enough for everyone to hear. I look around the room and everyone has tears. "Did you all hear that? I'm getting married to the most wonderful woman God could have picked for me."

"Woooohoooo!" I yell, finally letting out all the stress I'd been holding in from all the planning for the last few months. But I'd been dreaming of it for about a year and half now it was coming true. Dad gets up from his chair and congratulates us, and Mom follows, as does the rest of the family.

Mom, yells out, "I am getting another bottle of champagne to make a toast." Everyone gets a glass of champagne and Dad makes a toast as the man of the house.

"Lacy, I have known you a little while, but I have never seen my son this happy before in my life. I know you are the one for him, and I see the strength you both share as a team never let that team work end. Derek, son you are a gift to your mother and I, we know you have chosen a perfect woman for you. Your mother and I wish you many long years of love, joy, happiness, ends to fights with long make-ups, and grace to never give up on each other no matter what you go through. Cheers to unconditional love, friendship, and years of happiness together."

Lacy and I say thank you at the say time.

"Oh, and Lacy, I am Dad to you now."

"Yes, Dad"

"And I'm Mom." Mom says, as she comes over to give Lacy a hug and kiss on each cheek. I couldn't of asked for a more beautiful evening. For not knowing what I was doing I sure pulled it off, too bad my best friend was not here to see it in action. We all help clean-up, it was time to

The Disturbed

go to bed, I didn't feel right leaving Lacy down stairs, now she was my bride to be, and I wanted to be close to her. Mom saw us on the stairs saying our goodnights and said,
"Oh, go on, you are almost married, now hurry up before I change my mind." You'd never seen me run up those stairs so fast since I've lived there. I held Lacy in my arms all night. We talked about dates and I asked her what she thought about Valentine's day of this year. She looked at me with a grin and said,
"I'm not too sure, that is a big love day who would want to get married on a day of love…" I kiss her on the lips, knowing that was another 'Yes.'
"So, does that mean yes?"
"Yes, that means yes."
"You know that means our anniversary will be on February 14th, every year now."
"Yep!"
I desired to make love to her, but really just wanted to hold her that night. There was no better feeling at that moment then knowing she was mine, and she said 'Yes,' life just seemed perfect.

Christmas morning was here, and the smell of pancakes, coffee, Christmas tree filled the whole house, and man was I one happy dude. Mom, let Lacy and I cuddle lastnight, so I got to wake-up to her in my arms as well. Just as I rolled over and started kissing her all over I hear

Mom, "Derek, Lacy, Christmas Breakfast is ready. I get up and open the door, "Be right down Mom." We got our robes on and start down the stairs and all I feel is warmth and excitement in my heart. We enjoyed our breakfast and we were all ready to open the rest of the presents. Dad decided to get a fire going while Lacy and I helped Mom clean-up a bit so we could get to making another mess now in the living-room from all the wrapping-paper. I got on the floor next to the tree as everyone took a seat near the tree.

"Hey Derek, wait a minute before you start opening gifts I want to shoot some video of everyone okay. Go ahead and hand one out, I'll be right back, going to grab a couple of logs for the fire."

"Okay Dad, you need a hand with that?"

"Nope, I got it, just be a minute."

"Okay, we'll wait for ya."

I watch Dad head out the side-door. I knew he would not be gone too long because there were already cut wood logs stack near the back shed. I go to check on Dad and I see him enter the shack. I was thinking to myself that is weird, the wood is outside the big shed. I figured he just needed a tool or something. I go back to the Christmas tree and sit down waiting for Dad to walk in any minute.

The Disturbed

Dad

"Why is this shed-door opened? What the hell? Jazz? What are you doing in here son? I thought you would have come in the house or something. What's up with the mask and why are you dressed like that? You are the one who has been stalking Derek haven't you? You are the one setting him up and ruining his life!"

"You were not supposed to find out about me. Why did you have to come in here old man? I didn't want you to get involved."

"Get involved in what? Jazz what are you doing? Please don't! What the hell is wrong with you?"

"Shut-up old man before they come out here! You were never supposed to get in the way. I am sorry, but you cannot send me to jail, you just can't, I won't let you, Derek, has always had a fucking perfect life, I've been sick of Derek's perfect life since we were kids and I've hated him for it. Well fuck him and fuck you!"

"Uah, Uah, Uah, auucann't bre……."

"I've been sitting under this Christmas tree a while now, Dad sure is taking a long time. I'll go see if he needs any help out there." I get up from underneath the tree to go check on him. Maybe he can't carry all the wood, I should have gone with him. I get to the shed and find the door still open and call for Dad. There's no answer, so I go inside and find my Dad on the floor. What the hell! Dad?

231

Dad? He doesn't respond at all. Oh, fuck I have to call for Mom for help.

"Mom!!!" I check for a pulse and I can't find one, so I start CPR. Just then Mom gets to the shed-door.

"Oh my God Derek, what happened? Is he breathing?"

"Mom call 911 NOW!"

Mom's on the phone with 911, telling the dispatcher that Dad was found on his back in the backyard shed, while I'm losing it trying so hard to stay focused on counting knowing my Dad's heart had stopped. I can't help but think what the hell happened to him as I try and save his life. I love this man and all he has ever been to me, he's my Pop.

"The paramedics are on the way Derek, keep trying son." Mom, comes down to the floor with me and starts to cry frantically, realizing that her husband is not breathing and is on the ground in the shed on Christmas Day. I keep checking for a pulse and there is none.

"Come one Dad, I need you. Please don't leave us now, not today, not like this."

The paramedics arrive and take over the CPR, they try the defibrillator and it doesn't work either. I try and comfort Mom as best as I could, but she was inconsolable.

"Derek, what are we going to do? Why won't he wake-up? What happened son?"

"I don't know Mom, I came out to check on him, and found him on the ground."

"Oh, my God, Derek, I can't live without your father Derek, he has to be okay."

"I know Mom, I'm sure they are doing all they can." I tried to stay calm, but inside I feared the worst.

"All we can do is pray now Mom. I'm sorry I yelled at you Mom."

"Derek, I understand." She takes my face in her hands as if to say I know you are doing your best, without even saying a word.

Lacy and the rest of the family come rushing out realizing that the paramedics stopped at our house. "Christmas is on hold until further notice. Dad's not breathing." I tell the family all at once, there was no sense in hiding it, this was our reality right now, and they had a right to know.

"Everyone please pray, Derek can you and Lacy come with me to the hospital?"

"Absolutely Mom, we will meet you there."

"Thank you, son, I know how hard that must have been on you finding your father like that alone."

"Yeah Mom, I will never forget it."

"I'm riding with Dad okay son."

"We will follow you Mom."

We get to the hospital and they ask all of us to wait in the waiting room. I am pacing back and forth. Mom is rocking in the seat probably not realizing it while she stares at the TV not even paying attention to the program on, just a blank stare. I think to myself, maybe I should go sit by her, my pacing is probably making things worse. Lacy not knowing how to console either one of us asks if we want something from the gift shop to drink:

"Can I go get you some coffee or something to drink?"

"Not for me hon, what about you Mom?"

"No Derek, not right now son. Thank you."

We wait for what seems like days, but it's been about an hour. Just then the doctor comes out, and the look on his face is not good.

"Holson family?"

"Yes."

"I am so sorry to have to tell you this but Mr. Holson did not make it. He had a massive heart attack, and there was nothing we could do."

Mom, yells, "No!" as she falls into my arms, my grasp keeps her from falling to the ground.

"Can we spend some time with him please?"

"Yes, family is able to spend as much time as they need after they have lost a loved one, I am so sorry for your loss, if you would like to be with him now I can escort you there."

The Disturbed

"Yes, please, is that okay with you Mom?" Mom can't speak she just nods her head giving me a yes on going in to basically say goodbye to Dad. I can't believe this is happening. I just proposed to my beautiful now soon to be wife and lost my Dad all within twenty-four hours. What the hell is going on? On Christmas day? How could I ever console Mom? I was so glad Lacy and I were here during this time and not in Alabama, I do not think Mom could have handled that, not that she can handle it happening now. I just could not see her having found him by herself. Lacy and I were meant to be here for sure.

We walk in the room slowly pulling back the curtain. We see Dad laying there pale and lifeless. Mom walks over to him slowly and lays across his chest.

"Oh, Henry, why did you have to go? You are my world Mr., what am I supposed to do without you?" I wanted Mom to say whatever she felt. I was not going to interrupt her now. This was her time, that was her soul-mate, her everything as much as Lacy was mine. I couldn't watch without having tears run down my cheek.

"Mom, would you like sometime alone with Dad?"

"It's okay Derek, I would say everything the same if you were not here and I want you to be close during this time as well. I think we are all going to need each other to get through the Christmases from now on."

"I agree with you on that Mom." She was right, our lives had changed forever and Christmases and cabin trips would never be the same after this day. I walk over and grab my Dad's hand for the last time. I couldn't hold back the tears now, it hit me all at once. I guess I was holding up until then. Lacy came to my side and gently put her hand on my back to let me know she was there. All I could think is what the hell? For some reason, I felt the same way as I did when the incident happened in Alabama, dazed. This was far more important, and a far more deeper tragedy, but the way I was reacting was with pure shock and disbelief. I wanted Dad back, Mom wanted Dad back. How were we going to get past this and go home without him?

Hours pass like minutes, and it's time to go home without the man who had taught me how to be a man. I hold Mom close as I walk her out to the reception area.

"Excuse me." I say to the receptionist sitting in front of me.

"Yes, how can I help you?"

"My father passed away today and I wanted to let the hospital know we would be making arrangements for him later tonight and will phone the hospital with the information tomorrow morning. First name Henry, last name is Holson." As Dad's name comes out of my mouth it seemed to drive the nail in a bit deeper. I hold Mom a bit tighter as I hear her sob.

"Oh, I'm so sorry for your loss, that will be fine. Thank you for letting us know."

"Thank you."

We walk toward the car all of us numb, not saying a word, as if we were all just able to communicate without words our complete sadness of the day, and the months to come learning how to live without Dad. I felt like I had to fill Dad's shoes now. I just felt like I needed to take up the responsibility at least until Mom was stronger. So, I decided to tell the rest of the family in person not over the phone. All the way home I thought to myself how do I ask Mom about arrangements; how could I even bring myself to talk about that right now? I wanted to give her this day before I even mentioned it to just be. We got home and told the rest of the family that was at the house and they helped comfort Mom. Lacy and I got to be alone for a while, she grabbed me, and I fell apart in her arms. She had seen me go through so much shit, but this hit me harder than anything I had ever been through. She held me while I cried, and I was so thankful my Dad got to meet her and see us get engaged. I knew he'd be watching us get married too somehow, that's how Dad was, not even death could keep him away from what he loved. I truly believed he was with us still, just in a different way. I blow my nose and look into Lacy's eyes.

"Thank you for being here babe, I could not do this without you."

"Derek, I was meant to be here."

"I don't know how or when to bring up arrangements for Dad with Mom. I know I have to but she's hurting and I just don't know when it's the right time babe."

"Derek, there will never be a right time. Mom, is going to hurt regardless of you bringing up arrangements for Dad or not. But what will help is maybe giving her today, and then working on closure. As hard as it will be Derek, you both will have to accept what has happened, be thankful for all the time you did have together, grieve, and let him go, so y'all can heal."

"You're right Lacy. Hey, I want to go back to the shed for a few minutes okay, if you don't mind hon?"

"Derek, go…don't worry about me right now. I will see if Mom would like anything to eat or drink and just be with her okay."

"Thank you, Lac."

I go back to the shed and tears are still running down my face as I get closer to where Dad was. I couldn't help but think over and over again what the hell Mom and I will do without Dad. He was the strong tower of this family,

The Disturbed

now I had to be strong for Mom, could I? Although I questioned myself I knew now I wasn't alone anymore either. I had Lacy and we all had each other, Dad would expect me to man up for Mom and be her strength. I guess that's why I had to go back to the shed alone. To get that strength he left right here for me. I said my goodbye, collected it, and went back in the house. The police said they didn't find any foul-play at the residence. I over-heard the family talking, at least the family was talking about it, and not keeping it all bottled-up inside like I had.

"Anyone need anything to drink or eat? I know we may not feel like eating but Dad would want us to keep enjoying life, and take care of ourselves you know."
 "You're right Derek, I'll have some tea, son." Mom said. Boy was I glad to hear that out of her. I think Dad left some strength behind just for her as well because I just saw it kick-in.

The coroner recorded the cause of death as a massive heart attack, but it did say that there was some bruising around my father's neck; however, when we asked about this we were told it was not uncommon when someone cannot breathe. Although, he did say that many victims of a heart attack may be likely to grab their chest. This didn't bring anymore comfort but it was closure that we all needed now. Lacy and I approached Mom the next morning asking where she wanted Dad to be buried. She said they had plots already, and had a place they both decided on. Mom told me they did this so I would never have to worry about what to do for them, and what each other would have wanted as well. Mom didn't get much sleep, but I didn't blame her, I actually think no one in the house slept well under the circumstances we were hit with on Christmas day. The gifts were still all under the tree, it was as if Christmas was just stopped for eternity.

Mom, gave me the information and asked if I would call and ask for Dad's body to be picked-up, that everything was already payed for. I get off the phone from making the hardest call of my life and I hear the doorbell ring. I look through the peephole and see it's Jazz. I open the door.

"Hey Derek, sorry I missed Christmas man, I just got into town last night. Mom said she has gotten me something special a week ago and I got to thinking how much I miss home and hangin with you guys."

"Jazz, glad to see you man, but I have some bad news. My Dad passed away yesterday."

"What? On Christmas day? How?"

"Come in, have a seat man. He passed away from a massive heart attack."

"Holy crap man, I'm sorry. Is there anything I can do?"

The Disturbed

"Not really, I will be with Mom and Lacy for a while. Really want to stay close to home and Mom, you know."

"Yeah, yeah, sure, that's understandable man. So, did you guys get engaged?"

"Yes, we did and I am so grateful Dad was here for that, and he sure loved Lacy. I know I will feel his presence when we get married in February."

"Yeah man, I am sure he his spirit will be around for that special day. Hey, I'm going to take off okay, I want to give you time with you family to grieve. Stop by when you feel like it, okay man?"

"Yeah, sure thanks, and I'll let you know when the funeral is if you want to go."

"Yeah, let me know, I'll come man."

"Okay, talk to you later then."

"Alright, later." Jazz walks out the door and closes it behind him. I can't help but think that it seems unlike him to leave in a moment like this. But I guess death makes a lot of people uncomfortable. I would have probably done the same thing, I guess.

The mortuary called and said that they had a couple of dates to choose from for Dad's funeral. It was not something we wanted to deal with, but it was time to decide what day we would lay Dad to rest.

"I'm sorry, can you please hold on a moment."

"Sure, no problem."

"Mom, they want us to choose a day for the funeral, here is a calendar."

"Derek, get that calendar out of my face! I'm not ready! I'm just not ready!"

Mom, runs out of the room heading upstairs. My heart sinks almost to where I can't breathe. I want to comfort her, but I don't think anyone can right now, which is completely understandable. I decide to make the date for as far out as I can.

"Hello sir, we would like to make it for the furthest date possible."

"Yes sir, that would be this Saturday sir, will this date be alright for the family?"

"Yes sir, please book it for this Saturday."

"Yes sir, it is done, do you have any questions for me."

"No, that would be all, thank you."

"Yes, thank you."

I hung up the phone and wanted to go talk to Mom, but at the same time I just felt she needed some time to process what was happening and how her life was forever changed. I wrote down the date on the calendar, but felt unready myself. How the fuck does anyone get ready for something like this? How the fuck was Mom ever going

The Disturbed

to be ready for something like this? I was hurting just like Mom, and this time not even Lacy could take away this pain. Later that evening I had a chance to talk to Mom, we cried, we laughed, we reminisced about old times, we shared the pain like no one else could. I saw another side of Mom that evening, I guess you can say I grew into my role of father of the house.

Saturday morning came, we were as ready as we could be for a day like this. Most of our family showed up, Jazz was there along with his family. Priest Jenkins, was a long-time friend of Dad's and the family did Dad's funeral. It was a sad day, but also a day of closure. I stayed behind and said some final words to Dad, while I leaned on the coffin. I had to let him know what he meant to me even though I felt he was not there in body, but free with God somehow. I knew he was listening, and that was all that mattered. After the funeral we all went back to the house for some food and fellowship, which I believe Mom really needed that day. It was a day I would never forget. I believed it was the day I truly become the man that Dad had wanted me to be; however, I never thought something like this would make me see it.

CHAPTER 11

Truth Exposed

Two weeks had passed, and we were all still feeling the blow of losing Dad so soon. Lacy and I had stayed really close to Mom the whole time even though I knew deep inside there was no way to really take away the pain she was feeling, or I was feeling, but time. I knew we would always miss him but the house was not the same without him. We didn't dare talk about the cabin. I was sure we would not visit that place for a long while, not even Lacy and I. For the first two weeks, it seemed as if Mom sometimes forgot that Dad was gone. I would see her fixing him a plate of food or start to call out his name only to realize again he was never coming back. She broke down a few times when she realized it,

I knew there was nothing I could do but let her grieve and be there as much as I could.

Lacy was busy learning a new cooking recipe from Mom, so I thought I would go over to see Jazz, I hadn't seen him since the funeral, which was a bit odd to me. I mean I didn't want to be babied or anything, but he was my best friend I thought he would have checked up on me or something. I figured I would go over there and see what's up; I needed to get out of the house, seeing a good friend would do me some good right now.

"Lacy, Mom, I'm going to go over and see Jazz for a few. You don't mind, do you?"

"I don't mind son, go ahead, Lacy?"

"Sure hon, have a good time, Mom and I are cooking up something good in here. Besides I'm nervous with you here watching me learn how to cook. I would rather show you my skills later." I go to Lacy, give her a kiss on the cheek, and Mom as well.

"I'll be right back, I don't plan on staying too long, mainly want to see what's up with him and why he has not called or come by."

I pull-up to Jazz's house and he's outside washing his car. Something I have been needing to do for a while now.

"Hey, what's up?"

The Disturbed

"Not much…Just missing my Dad and thought I would come see what you are up to."

"Not a lot as you can see. Want to do something later? Maybe a movie or skate park?"

"Yeah, that sounds cool."

"So, how have you been anyway?"

"You know, it's been hard…I mean, I think everyone at the house is still not used to not having Dad around. I still look for him to be in his recliner-chair all the time. Mom had called his name a couple of times when it's time to eat. It's been rough."

"I can imagine. I'm sure it will take a while to get back to normal or realizing he is not there anymore. I really am sorry for your loss Derek."

"Thanks, man…that means a lot. Hey, I will let you go, you mind if Lacy comes with tonight?"

"No problem, you guys are onesies now right." I give him a big grin.

"Yep, I guess we are. Hey thanks for being there for me. See you a bit later, let me know when you are ready to go. Do you know about what time?"

"How about, seven o'clock or so?"

"Cool, we will be ready with freakin bells on." I laugh out loud. I have to admit it was probably the first time I had laughed since Dad died, and it felt good.

I get back home and Lacy and Mom had made an amazing lunch. We all sat at the same table and talked a lot about Dad. We laughed, cried, were silent, then we would remember something else, laugh, cry, and be silent all over again. We were healing together I guess, we sure all needed it and the togetherness. I had asked Lacy about going to the movies later that night, and she was all for it. Leaving Mom alone was so hard for me. I didn't know how to feel when I did. I guess I felt guilty. Mom didn't mind, she always said she needed some time alone too to talk to Dad, and just heal. I was not sure if that was true, or if she was trying to prevent herself from feeling guilty if we stayed home, or me from feeling guilty if I went. Mom had always been very strong, she was holding-up well now too.

We ended up going with Jazz to the movies. It was hard at first, I couldn't stop thinking if Mom was okay or if she was just sitting there crying. She was right though, she needed that time alone to learn to be alone again. The only way to heal from Dad's passing was to feel the pain, and I knew that. It didn't make it easier though, that's for sure. Lacy and I enjoyed the movie, it was kind of too space-ish for my liking but Lacy liked it. I mean I had a thing for the big movies like 'Star Trek' and 'Star Wars' but I was not a space fanatic by any means.

There was no celebration with the family having Dad's funeral at the start of the new year. We all missed Dad so much. I had gone back to work, Lacy had gone back

The Disturbed

to school after a couple more weeks but it just was not the same without Dad, nothing was. The one big positive thing was we were planning a wedding, which I knew Dad would want us to be doing. He was happy for us when we got engaged on Christmas Eve, and I just knew he would be there on that special day. We had planned to get married on Valentine's Day just as I had hoped, Lacy was excited. We were already at the end of January, so it was coming up soon. Lacy and I decided to live with Mom for a while as a family, it felt like the right thing to do for now at least. I knew eventually we would branch off into our own home, but now was not the time; it was time for family, and bonding. Mom and Lacy did most of the planning which made them happy, so it made me happy. I would occasionally be asked what I thought about a color or something like that, then be shown what the plans were and every time I loved all of them. They had gotten done with the invitations already and had asked me to take one to Jazz. I guess they saw I needed to get out of the house a bit too. The delusions have not been bothering me much lately, maybe because I have been so focused on so many other things, I sure wondered about that. I thought maybe it was the medications working finally, I didn't really know, but I was glad they were not as frequent.

The day of the wedding was here, I was nervous as shit, but happy as all hell. This was it, I was marrying my queen. The one woman who had been with me, and stayed with me through everything. It was time to make her mine, and I knew Dad was here. Lacy looked so absolutely beautiful in her lacy gown from head to toe, she was jaw dropping gorgeous. I never wanted to forget this moment. I wanted lots of pictures, but it was like I didn't want this moment to end.

The whole ceremony was beautiful. Lacy had chosen white and a violet purple for the decorations. Her father walking her down the aisle just as she wanted. Jazz was my best man as we planned. Although, it was a bit out of the norm, Mom, saved a chair for Dad, which touched everyone's heart. Before the wedding we flew Lacy's parents out to stay with us for the wedding and to stay a couple of days to enjoy Big Bear.

It was nice to have the family around, but I felt a need to get away for a while, and go see what Jazz was up to. It was about four days since the wedding, Lacy's parents had gone back to Alabama, and I wanted to invite him back over for some food, and family time. I guess I wanted his to know even though I was married he was still my bud. We would still be hanging out and doing stuff together. We never talked about all of that. I went up to Lacy and told her I was going to go invite Jazz over for some food and family time. I just felt like maybe he was feeling like an outcast or something. I mean he hardly called anymore, so I guess I felt I needed to check on him. I kiss Lacy and Mom on the cheek, letting them know I would be right back.

Last Visit to Jazz

I get to Jazz's house, but don't see his car. I go to the door and knock. Jazz's Mom answers.

"Oh, hey Derek, how have you been son? I'm so sorry for your loss. Jazz said he wanted to give you some time to heal before he came by again. He's not here, but you are welcome to wait up in his room if you like he said he'd be back in a few minutes."

"Okay, no problem Miss K."

"I'm sure he'll be right back."

I get up in Jazz's room and I throw myself on his red beanbag chair. I can't help but think about all we had been through and how long we had known each other. I guess Dad's passing really made me appreciate things a lot more. Time seemed to be so fleeting to me now after losing Dad. I look around the room at all the clutter and my eye stops on something I see across the room. I get up from the beanbag chair, and walk over to a pile of clothes scattered all over the floor near the closet. I bend down to get a closer look and I see it. It's the fucking mask and jacket I have always seen the faceless fuck wearing, even though I never was up close to his face enough to truly make out what the hell was wrong with it, I know something was, now I knew what. Now I knew who. Oh, fuck Jazz? He has been stalking me all this fucking time? What the fuck is going on? Oh, SHIT! I hear the front screen door slam shut, and then I hear Jazz's Mom yell from the other room. I cover up the mask, and jacket as if I had not seen shit, scrambling to sit back down in the beanbag chair across the room. Slowing my breathing as fast as I can to seem calm.

"Jazz, Derek is waiting for you in your room son."

"Okay, thanks Mom." I hear Jazz say as he hurries up the stairs.

"Hey Derek, what the hell are you doing here?"

"Hey man, sorry, your Mom said I could wait in your room. I didn't think you'd mind at all. I mean I've sat in here before by myself. What's up with you man, you alright?"

"Yeah, I'm fine, I've just been really busy. I have a lot to do today maybe I can stop by later?"

"Okay, yeah sure…I was just about to leave anyway, I have to get back home, Lacy and Mom need me to go with them somewhere. It was nice seeing you man. Hope you, and your Mom are doing well. If you ever need anything call me."

"Okay thanks, talk with you later."

"Okay sure." I hurry out of there as fast as I can. I have to get to Lacy, to tell her what I saw. This is the break I have been needing, although it shocks me to my core.

I am passing the speed limits I know, but I need to get home. I rush inside the house, Lacy and Mom looking at me with their eyes wide open in shock.
"Derek, what is going on?"
"Mom, I have to talk to Lacy alone for a moment please it's very important."
"Okay, son go right ahead."
I take Lacy up to our room, she's asking me all the way up the stairs what is wrong. She's frantic to know why I'm so on edge. I sit her down on our bed.
"Lacy, you know I went to Jazz's house right?"
"Yeah babe, but…"
"Wait, just hear me out okay."
"Okay hon."
"I showed up at his house and he wasn't there, so his Mom told me to wait for him in his room as I have always done. So, I go up there and sit in the beanbag chair I always chill in while waiting for him or even visiting, right. I look over at a pile of clothes he has on the floor close to his closet and I see the mask and jacket that I have seen the faceless fuck wear for the last couple of years."
"Oh my God, Derek!"

"I know, it has been Jazz this whole time and I never suspected him at all. I mean he would be moody and weird off and on but that was always Jazz. But that time he came on to you I was feeling something was not right with him though, but I just didn't listen to my gut, Lacy."

"Well, babe you have known him for so long, I don't think you would suspect him either, nor would I think you would want to due to the fact you have known him for so long and you both grew, up together. What are we going to do hon? I mean this means he is responsible for beating your skull in with a pipe too."

"Lacy, I think he may be responsible for a whole lot more than that."

"Well, the first thing I want to do is go talk to my therapist to see what she tells me. I want her to know this has not been a delusion, but it had been real this whole time. I want to go to the police but I'm thinking they may not do anything because he has never been seen stalking me or trying to kill me. Basically, I have no evidence to prove this right now, so I don't want you or Mom to say a word of any of this okay. I want you both act the same around Jazz unless he tries to hurt you or something, so we can catch him. I'll go downstairs and tell Mom the same thing okay."

"Okay babe, be careful and hurry home soon."

"I will, come with me down-stairs."

I go up to Mom and quickly explain what I had just told Lacy and for her to continue to treat Jazz as always. Jazz didn't know I knew and I didn't want to lead on that I knew at all.

I call Dr. Searian to see if she could fit me in for an appointment right away, I tell her it's urgent something I have never done before. Not ever after I got back here and had lost everything but Lacy. She says she can fit me in if I come in now. I was so relieved because I needed to talk about this bad, I need direction of some kind.

I show up at her office, took a seat until she came out to get me. Just as I go to pick-up a magazine to read while I wait I see her coming down the hall.

"You ready?"
"Sure am."
"Great. Come on back."

We walk back to her office she tells me to take a seat anywhere feels comfortable. I sit down feeling like I want to start talking already, but I wait for her to ask me why I'm here.

"So, Derek, what's going on? You said this is urgent?"
"Yes, very urgent. Do you remember when I mentioned I believed someone had been following me?"

"Yes, I do. I have many notes about our discussions on this problem you were having, is it still happening?"

"It's not only still happening, but I found out who it is. It's my friend who I have known most of my life, Jazz."

"Are you sure he's been stalking you?"

"I'm as sure of this as I am sitting here. I went to his house without calling. His mom told me he would be right back and that I could wait in his room if I wanted to, which I did. That's when I discovered the mask and jacket identical to what that faceless stalker had worn every time he showed up. I know it sounds like a lot to take in but I'm telling you the truth. I came here because I am not sure how to handle this. At this point I don't believe I have enough evidence to call the police on this, but when I do have evidence can you provide what I have shared with you to help my case?"

"Yes, I would be able to release it to your attorney with a signed release form, sure. I'm not sure how else I can help at this point Derek except to go to the police with it, and see if they can question him maybe he will stop."

"Yeah, but he's not just responsible for stalking me, he also tried to kill me in Alabama. All his strange behavior is starting to make a lot more sense to me now that's for sure. I'm also wondering if he had anything to do with my father's death. I know that is far-fetched, but it's in my mind that's for sure."

The Disturbed

"Well, Derek, all I can suggest is to go to the police and make a report, ask them to check it out. I'm not saying I don't believe you, but there is not a lot I can do at this point."

"Okay, I wanted to tell you I knew more and I wanted you to at least document that in case I need any of this later. I don't what to do either except wait to see if it happens again."

"Derek, make sure you stay safe, and don't take matters into your own hands."

"That's a hard one to not think about. I just wish for once someone would believe me."

"Derek, I didn't say I don't believe you, I just am not sure you have enough evidence yet to do anything. That's all I'm saying."

"Okay, I will make an appointment for next week maybe I will have more information by then."

"Okay, sounds good, Derek, I'm here to help anytime. See you at your next appointment."

"Alright, see you then."

I make my appointment, and drive back home feeling lost. I'm thanking God I have Lacy to go home to because a lot of the time she brings me so much strength. I get home, her and mom are not there. I go upstairs for a nap. I have to work tomorrow and it's been one hell of a day.

Lacy and Mom

"Hey Mom, I believe I may need a test."

"A test? Aww, Lacy, really?"

"Well, I'm not sure, but it's worth a test anyway. I'm late about two weeks, and while we're here I should probably get one. I think Derek would be thrilled, and he needs some good news right now."

"Yes, he sure does Lacy, he sure does."

I wake to the sound of the door opening, and knowing the frame of mind I'm in now I had to make sure Mom and Lacy are safe. I can see from upstairs it's them and I am relieved. I hear Mom yell up for me.

"Derek?"

"Yeah Mom, I'll be right down. I throw a shirt on and run-down stairs. I missed my Lacy even though we were apart just a couple of hours. I go to her and hug her tight. I tossed and turned the whole time I tried to take a nap so seeing her again sure calmed me.

"So, what did the therapist say babe?"

"Basically, she said I probably don't have enough evidence, and to not take matters into my own hands. But I'm not going to just take it if it happens again. I can't, I don't trust him now, and I have to protect you both, Dad would want me to."

The Disturbed

"Yes, Derek but he would not want you to put yourself in harm's way either, son."

"Your Mom's right Derek, please be careful, and don't do anything without thinking."

"I know, I know, I was lectured already thanks guys."

"Lacy and I will fix up some dinner you go relax son, we'll call you when it's ready."

"Thanks Mom, sorry if I seem on edge or am snapping, I don't mean to, I just am pretty pissed about this stalker asshole being my best friend, well was my best friend. It's going to be hard for me act like nothing's wrong if he comes by too but we still have to do that until I figure out what to do, okay?"

"Okay."

"Okay, Mom?"

"Alright son, I understand."

We all have a nice evening. Mom and Lacy made an amazing dinner as always. It was time for bed, and I was ready to hold my wife, and just let go of the day. Just before I doze off to sleep Lacy takes my hand and puts it on her belly. I think to myself that is weird, why is she doing that? Oh, maybe she's in the mood. Then she starts to move my hand in a circular motion now my brain is wondering what she is thinking. I turn to her and start to kiss her. She stops and looks me straight in the eyes while she is still moving my hand in the same place. Oh, my God! I think to myself.

"Lacy, are you trying to tell me something?"

"Ummhumm..."

"Oh, my God...are you? Are we?" She nods her head, "Yes"

"Yep, you're going to be a daddy, Derek." Wow! Shit just got beautifully real. I lay my head on her shoulder and begin to cry overwhelmed with joy. The last few months, needing to hear something so beautiful for so long and that was it. I start to kiss her all over, telling her how much I love her, and how happy I am.

"When did you find out?"

"Just today, hope you don't mind but Mom knows. I had to buy the test today and I didn't want to hide it from her. She said she knew you would be very excited."

"I'm one happy man that's for sure. I love you Lacy."

"I love you too Derek."

I hold her tightly, and we fall asleep in each other's arms.

"Uah Uah Uah! Oh God No!"

"Derek! Honey I'm right here. What's wrong?"

"Lacy, I had a dream that Jazz killed my father." I tell her barely able to catch my breath.

"Oh my God, I'm sorry hon, do you want to stay up a while?"

The Disturbed

"I can't go back to sleep like this right now. You rest I'm going to go get some milk and see if I can calm myself down."

"Well, I'm not going to be able to sleep without you, so can I go with?"

"Sure, come on. I sure love you Lac."

"Everything will work out babe, I promise. Do you really think Jazz could do a thing like that?"

"After him trying to kill me, I know he could, and I believe that dream is a sign. It was too real Lacy, way to real and it's something I want looked into as soon as this fucker gets close enough to me."

"Okay, babe I completely understand that. I will support you completely, okay?"

"Thanks babe." I kiss her on the forehead as just listening to her talk calms me down. I hated to be stalked all these years by this fucker, but I needed it to happen one more time. Something in me was taking no more bullshit from him. This time I was taking the fucker down. Lacy and I sit-up for about an hour drinking milk, while we dipped our cookies, talking about the new baby on the way, and trying to focus on the good that was happening in our life. Lacy had a way of bringing everyone up around her, no matter how she was feeling; she always had a smile on her face, and in her heart. This woman was my backbone, my strength, and my best friend. I thanked God for her. We go back up to bed, knowing I had to work in the morning again falling asleep holding each other close.

The alarm woke me up, I nearly smashed it the damn thing startled me so bad. I guess you can say I have been on edge lately, bad, trying not to take it out on any one I love. I turn over and Lacy is not there. I figure she is down stairs helping Mom with breakfast as always. I quickly go check on them, then come back up to shower, then it's off to work I go. I sure thank God for a great boss, who is kind and compassionate. He's really supported the family during the last couple of months and even gave me that raise he promised. I found myself praying more lately. Not that I still didn't cry every now and again, but I believed God was really blessing me and I knew this was all going to somehow work out. I knew Jazz had to get caught deep in my heart I knew God would help me. Maybe it was a feeling of Dad looking down on me, I knew he was with me and was rooting for me. Now I needed to make sure Dad wasn't murdered, but I knew I had help concerning that too, somehow, I just knew deep down.

As the day went on, I thought about the dream I had had last night almost more than Lacy telling me I was going to be a dad. I wanted to make sure my family would be safe when I was here at work. I thought about the notes that the coroner had written on Dad's death chart for

The Disturbed

the death certificate. Something inside told me Dad did not just have a heart attack. They never did an autopsy on Dad, but the notes stated bruising around the neck of my father, which would tell me he could not breathe, not just his heart was hurting him. I started to think about Lacy being pregnant more, and it was really sinking in. I was going to be a Dad, Lacy was having my baby. My dreams were finally coming true even in the mist of hell. I started to think about becoming a new father, and how I couldn't wait to get home to go over names with Lacy. It was about that time too, I got everything cleaned up, and clocked out.

I waved goodnight to my boss as I headed for the door to the parking lot. Employees were told to always park in the far back so the customers could use the closer parking, making it more convenient for them, which I didn't have a problem with at all. I make my way to my car just about three yards from it, and I see him. Oh, fuck yes, now is my chance, and he has no clue I know. I act like I'm afraid of him, but at the same time I don't take my eyes of him. He is not getting away this time. I get a bit closer to my car, drop my shit, and run after him. This fucker is not getting away from me now, my whole life is wrapped up in this, and it's coming to a close now. I tackle him down to the ground, he was not expecting it at all. We start fighting and I'm punching his face like there's no tomorrow, I take off his mask and look him straight in the eyes.

"You killed my father didn't you, you fuck face! You killed my Dad! You tried to kill me back in Alabama too. What the fuck is wrong with you? You're the one who is sick not me, you're the sick fuck!"

I beat the fuck out of him until I feel security pull me off him, it took two big guys to take me off him.

"Don't let that guy get away! He killed my father, and tried to kill me!"

"Didn't do shit to your father! Or you!"

"I work here, do not let that guy go nowhere!" I'm asking the security to bring my boss out here so I can tell him what just happened. The police show up, I give them a statement, and as much details as I can. Now I have some evidence, I have the mask, the jacket, and the man behind it all.

"Both of you have to come down to the station for holding. Derek, you for assault and Jazz for stalking until we can figure this whole thing out."

"Oh, what the fuck!"

"Watch your mouth, son."

"Sorry, officer this guy has made my life hell for almost three years, and he needs to pay for what he's done, and I want my family to be safe now. I just found out my wife is pregnant, and this guy already killed my

Dad, ruined my job, and life in Alabama, I didn't know it was him until recently. I just found the evidence to prove he was the one, but I never told him. I waited for him to try to stalk me again to scare me like he's done for years. This time I knew who it was, and I needed to catch him doing it so someone would believe me. Please if you would make a call to my therapist as well, she knows all about this. I really need someone to do an investigation about my father's death, and the attack on me in Alabama, he tried to kill me when I was at work."

"Okay, I understand you are upset, and you believe this man has hurt you, and your father. We will look into that, but for now I need to get all of your personal information, then we can take it from there."

"Thank you for listening."

I give him everything he asks for, and even offer information hoping they would hear me out. They take both me, and fuck-face Jazz down to the station, then put us in two different holding cells. After about an hour, I am told that my therapist wants to put me on a 5150 hold for seventy-two hours again. What the fuck, they don't fucking believe me? How am I going to fight or keep my family safe in there with nothing? At least it's not jail, but fuck this guy can't go free.

"Derek, your therapist does recommend us to send you to the psychiatric hospital to do an evaluation on you instead of processing you here. She had mentioned you had just seen her yesterday?"

"Yeah, I did."

"As far as Jazz is concerned we have to look into this further, but he will be held until the investigator gets in touch with him to ask him more questions. He will be kept here until he is arraigned within most likely two days, then the judge may have us hold him do to the evidence of the mask and the information you have given me."

"Please have the investigator come talk to me. I have a lot of information for him, and this is my life we are talking about here, as well as my family's. I am fearful for my family, and myself if he is let out I have no way to protect them, as I told you my wife is also pregnant, I just found out last night. Can I please make a phone call to my wife, I'm sure she is very worried about me right now."

"Yes, you can call right now. Ivan should be here to get you in about an hour I was told."

"Okay, thank you." I'm let out to make one call and it's to Lacy. She picks up and is frantic on the phone.

"Derek, what happened babe? Are you okay? Your boss called to check on us and told us what had happened."

"Listen babe, I'm okay, but they are going to put me on a hold at the psychic hospital until I can speak to this investigator, which is actually a good thing. I mean

The Disturbed

at least I will not be here at the jail. Lac, I had to attack him, I could not let him get away. I had no evidence, but now I do, I have something and it may be enough to make these people finally listen to me."

"Okay babe, I understand I just don't want you hurt. I need you, we need you."

"I know, I think everything is going to work out now okay. Please help Mom and pray this investigator listens to me. I have to go, I will call you as soon as I can, okay? I love you, Lacy."

"I love you too, Derek, I will be close to Mom and stay by the phone. I am praying a lot and will keep praying, okay? Stay strong Derek."

"I will, don't worry babe okay? I'll see you soon."

"Okay, see you soon." I hear her sobbing as I hang up the phone. I wish I was there, but at the same time I needed to do this. It may have been my only chance.

The psychiatric hospital van comes to get me, I am still in handcuffs, but they remove them just before I am put into the van. We get to the hospital and I am out in a room where I will stay until I am evaluated. I have been through this a few times so it's nothing new to me. Of course, I'm sure Jazz is the one who sent me here most of the time.

Jazz and the Investigator

"Hello, Jazz, my name is Detective Hughs. I'll be asking you some questions and it is vital that you are honest with me. You have been read your rights and this interview of questions will be videoed and audio taped. The sooner we can get through these questions the better it will be for both of us. I understand you haven't been arraigned yet, but as part of this on-going investigation and the allegations against you I must conduct this interview. Do you understand?"

"Yes, I understand."

"Here is some water, if you need a break anytime during the interview please feel free to let me know. Are we clear?"

"Yes, we are clear."

"Okay, first is there anything you would like to tell me before we begin?"

"Not really."

"Alright, Jazz did you move with Derek to Alabama approximately three years ago?"

"Yes, I did."

"Did you during this time or any time before or after stalk Derek?"

"A couple of times, yeah, but he deserved it."

"What do you mean by 'He deserved it?'"

"He just did."

"Why do you think he deserved it?"

"Because he had always had an easy life, and my life sucked. He always got the girl, he always had the nice car, the great parents, good grades, you name it, Derek was perfect."

"Do you have parents at home, or did you?"

"Yeah, my Dad left when I was born from what my Mom told me, I have a little sister who gets most of the attention, but I am a loner man."

"So, did you go with Derek to Alabama to purposely stalk him and make him think he was having delusions, or to worsen them?"

"I didn't think of it that way, but I guess I did, I was on auto-pilot man."

"Jazz do you do any type of drugs or do you drink?"

"Nope, no drugs, no alcohol. I mean once in a while I may have a beer."

"Okay, where were you on Christmas day between the hours of eight a.m. and nine p.m.?"

"I was in Alabama. Derek had asked me to come down for Christmas, but I told him I had to work. I had two jobs in Alabama. Then I spoke to my Mom who said she had a big gift for me and I missed them so I decided to drive back after Christmas."

"Were you anywhere near Derek's house or did you have any contact with Derek's father on Christmas day of 2016?"

"How could I if I was in Alabama?"

"I asked you a simple yes or no question. Please answer the question."

"No."

"Jazz did you at any time attack Derek in Alabama or try to hurt or injure him in any way?"

"Not that I recall. We lived together though."

"Jazz, do you have any history of mental disorders?"

"No, not that I know of. What does that got to do with anything? I know Derek does."

"Jazz, I just have a couple more questions for today. Those burn marks on your hands, how did you get them."

"Oh, these…I got them from work, I work at a gas station and someone threw a cigarette near the tanks…I got burnt putting the small fire out."

"Did you receive medical treatment for those burns?"

"Yes, I did. In Alabama, though."

"Okay Jazz, that will be all for now. I may come back to see you in a couple of days after you are arraigned."

"Why? I'm answering your questions."

"I am just doing my job Jazz."

Detective Hughs and the Police Department

"Well, guys, I think Derek may be on to something. I am not buying Jazz's story one bit. The guy sure has it out for Derek and bad. Don't let him go, I have a couple of

The Disturbed

places I need to research before I feel safe letting this kid out of here. There are too many suspicions, make sure he is held until this investigation is done. I may need a lie detector test done as well. I will catch up with you guys in a few days."

"Thank you, Detective Hughs."

"Yeah, thanks guys."

Derek

I've been at the psychic hospital two days now, was evaluated, they also called my therapist with their report on me. I am sitting in the room and finally a detective comes to see me. Oh man am I relieved to see him. I had just talked to Lacy, and she was on her way to speak with the therapist about the truth of this whole thing, and give her view point anyway.

"Good afternoon Derek, my name is Detective Hughs, with the Big Bear's Detective Bureau. How are you?"

"Well, to tell you the truth sir, I would much rather be home with my new wife with our baby on the way, but this needed to be done."

"That's understandable. Derek, I have to ask you a few questions and I need you to be a clear with me and honest as you can. Alright?"

"Absolutely. I have been waiting for you to come, I need someone to listen and care."

"Well, I am here to do just that Derek. Now, everything you say will be audio taped for my own reference as well as possible use of evidence in the court, do you understand?"

"Yes, sir."

"Can you tell me approximately how long you believe Jazz has been stalking you?"

"I would say I have been seeing this faceless guy for four years now. I guess towards the end of my last semester in college for my Bachelor's."

"How long have you been seeing your therapist Derek?"

"About five or six years off, and on. She knows all about my complaints about all of this and how I felt my being followed was real not just a delusion, but I am not sure if she believed me. That's been the problem, getting someone to listen to me, and not pass me off just because I had mental issues. I have been struggling with this for way too long now, and all I'm asking for is help to know the truth."

"That's what I am here to do Derek, and I will do my very best to get to the bottom of all of this, okay?"

"Thank you."

"Derek, I am reading notes here that say you were hit on the head, and someone was trying to kill you, whom you believe to be Jazz, correct?"

"Yes, I know who it was now because I showed up at his house unannounced, and his Mom told me to wait in his room for him as I had over the years. We were close like that. So I did, then I saw the mask and jacket there in a pile of clothes. I covered it up so he never knew I knew. But I went home and told my wife, and Mom not to act any different around him until he tried this again, and he did. That's why I'm here."

"So, you knew about the mask and jacket but you didn't come to the police?"

"No, I went to my therapist who said that it may not be enough evidence for the police to do anything. So, I did what I knew to do, and waited, while I tried to protect my family."

"Derek, the mask and jacket were they the same when you were assaulted in Alabama?"

"Yes, exactly the same. Before I knew who it was I, in self-defense set the person trying to kill me on fire, but the police say they never recovered a body so I started to think I was just going crazy, but I knew someone hit me, hit me hard, and I had proof of that."

"Derek, are you aware of the burn marks on Jazz's hands?"

"Yes, he mentioned it, but at the time I didn't think anything of it because he works at the gas station I got him a job at. He said he had burnt his hands and part of his arm putting out a fire at work. So, I guess I just let it go at the time. But I found out about his burns within days of what had happened to me, and I lost my job, almost my sanity, everything…thank God not my life. I mean Jazz had been my friend since we were kids, so I would not suspect him at all. That was when I decided to move back home with Mom and Dad."

"But, your Dad has since passed, right?"

"Yes, he passed away on Christmas morning while he was out getting firewood next to the shack out in back of the house."

"Okay, now was Jazz in California during this time?"

"Not that I know of, when I called he said he couldn't come down because he had to work. But, what was weird is that the day after my Dad had passed away, Jazz showed up at my house, and said he had just gotten into town."

"So, he said he wasn't coming then he shows up after your Dad passed away. Derek, your father passed away from a massive heart-attack, correct?"

"That's what they said, but the autopsy report said there were bruises around his neck, but the coroner said sometimes this is caused by the patient reaching for their neck when they can't breathe. I always questioned that though because it would seem that Dad would be grabbing his heart not his own neck."

"Okay, Derek, I will be doing an investigation on all of this. I need you to sign this release form to grant me access to all records pertain to your history in Alabama as well as California, as well as your mental health records from your therapists."

"No problem."

"Have you ever lived anywhere else Derek?"

"No, only here and Alabama."

"Okay, thank you for this vital information. I will keep in touch. You should hear from me with a week or so."

"Thank you Detective Hughs I really appreciate you looking into this, I believe this guy I have known all of my life since I can remember anyway tried to kill me and killed my father. This is why I had to attack him, it was my only chance to be heard."

"Okay, Derek, I will do my best to find out the truth. Take care of yourself, and your family okay?"

The detective leaves the room, and I sigh a sign of relief feeling as if someone is going to help me now. About a half an hour later a nurse comes in to let me know I would be going home in the late evening and if there was someone I preferred them to call to pick me up. I told them to phone my wife, and she would come get me. I was glad I only had a few more hours to go, and I was also glad that someone was investigating this whole thing. I guess I felt relieved, happy, and I sure missed Lacy.

Lacy came to pick me up, it was about ten o'clock p.m., but I didn't mind, I just wanted to go home. I wanted to see my wife. Lacy told me as soon as she saw me that they were still holding Jazz, pending the investigation, that the judge did order it. Oh yes, this is what I wanted to hear. She said she had also spoken with my therapist, she said the therapist had received a call from the detective, and would be speaking with him later in the week. Lacy could obtain information about me because I had signed a release form for her to access my records any time after we were married. I had nothing to hide from her, and she had nothing to hide from me. We got home, and went to sleep. We both missed each other, but I think we were too mentally worn out to be romantically involved right now.

Early the next morning I called my boss to ask if it was okay to come to work, and went back to work that morning, having the best day ever. I just felt free from concern, safe knowing Jazz the faceless fuck was in jail. I was having a baby, and felt my family was safe as well. Life just felt good. I was waiting to hear back from the investigator still, but knew he would find something. Lacy had made a baby doctor appointment to see how far along she was, and made an ultrasound appointment. Of course, that was one appointment I was not going to miss. I was really thankful of what God was doing in my life. I could see how He was taking care of all the things I had no clue of how to, and I was grateful.

A few more days go by, and now it's been about two weeks since I've heard anything about the investigation from Detective Hughs, and finally I get a call from Lacy at work.

"Derek, sorry to bother you at work babe, but the detective called and he wants to meet with you, he has some news."

"You never bother me, call me whenever you want Lac, I love you honey. You are the reason I am at this place anyway, you, and junior." I tell her with a perma-grin. "Okay, I will give him a call right now on my lunch. Thanks baby. I'll see you when I get home okay?"

"Okay babe, I love you talk to you soon."

"Talk to you soon."

I get off the phone with Lacy and call Detective Hughs.

"Hello, may I speak with Detective Hughs please?"

"This is he, how may I help you?"

"Hello Detective Hughs, it's Derek Holson, returning your call sir."

"Yes, Derek, I wanted to know if you will have time to sit down and speak with me about this case. I believe I have some good and bad news for you. Would you be available this evening perhaps?"

"Sure, anytime sir, can my wife be present with me when you let me know?"

"I don't see a problem with that at all. How does six o'clock sound? I can come to your home to make it more convenient for you."

"Six o'clock is fine for me too. I will be there sir. Thank you, Detective Hughs."

"Alright, I will see you then, you're welcome Derek and thank you for your cooperation in this matter, I'm sure it's been hard on you, and your family."

"Yes, sir."

"Okay, see you this evening six o' clock sharp."

"See, you then."

I hang-up the phone, and I just know he has something good to say to me. I work my shift, now it's time to close-up shop. I can't wait to get home to my Lacy and hear what Detective Hughs has to say. I know he said there is some bad news he has to tell me as well, but I am trying to focus on the positive for now. Six o'clock rolls around, as I see his car pull up near the curb, my heart races feeling the need to know what he has to say. As he walks up to the door I watch every foot step as if it were my last breath. Lacy and I greet him at the door.

"Hello Detective Hughs, thank you for coming."

"No need for thanks, I'm merely doing my job."

The Disturbed

"Please come in and have a seat."

"Would you like something to drink?" Mom says, as she is always the best hostess.

"Detective Hughs, I hope you don't mind if my Mom is present while you talk to us."

"I don't mind; however, what I have to say to you is highly sensitive. So, please know you must be ready to hear whatever I have to say."

"Mom?"

"I'm okay Derek, I want to know."

"Let me start by saying, thank you for allowing me to be welcomed into your home. I have both good news and bad news as I told Derek this afternoon on our phone conversation. The good news is that I do not think Jazz will be getting out anytime soon. I have done a lot of research both here and have also obtained information pertaining to this case in Alabama. We had also gotten a search order after I had found information confirming what Derek had told me had happened in Alabama, and I was also able to find receipts of dates when Jazz, arrived here back in California. I was able to obtain the police reports from that day, as well as your hospital records. I also obtained records on the hospital records of Jazz, which were on the very same day from a hospital quite a few miles away from the city called Wellington in which you both lived, and worked as well as where

279

he said the accident happened. I was able to obtain receipts from his move back here to California which was five days before Christmas day. I have as evidence the mask, jacket, and notes of plans he had and times he had stalked you, along with the times he had stalked you tracing back years as you also told me about Derek. I spoke to your therapist, Derek, in great detail about how you have struggled over the years and why you decided to move. Unknowingly taking the very issue you were trying to get away from with you in the same car. However, as you said he had been your best friend for many years so why would you suspect him at all."

"That's exactly right."

"We also did a lie detector test on Jazz concerning both the attack on you in Alabama Derek, as well as the possible attack on your father. This is very hard for me to say, but your father was murdered. Jazz failed the lie-detector test as well."

"Oh, my God!" I hold Mom close to me, feeling my heart sinking into my stomach.

"The good news is we got him, he has both in recording and in writing confessed to all the crimes, and you were right about everything you shared with me Derek. The bad news is we can't bring your father back, but please take comfort in knowing there is closure here and I do believe your father, and mother, know you worked hard to make that happen, and the truth had now protected the rest of your family, and possibly many more people. Jazz is very mentally sick, but he is off the streets now, and will stay off the streets."

"Wow! You sure were not kidding about good, and bad news. This is definitely bitter-sweet, but so needed. We will have to heal again, I think, in a whole new light. Mom, you okay?"

"I'm okay son, I'm so proud of you, and I know your father is too, you better believe that son."

"You will not need to testify because we have his confessions as well as the evidence needed, but this case is already a pretty much open and shut case. There will be a sentencing court date if you would like to attend this. He left a trail of evidence as if he thought no one would even think he is capable of doing anything like this, but the managing of your disorders Derek is what ultimately helps this case the most, because you were determined despite them to make a better life for yourself, and now you can. I am very sorry for your family's loss, and that we have angels watching over us up there. I'm proud of you as well Derek for not giving up in the mist of the hell you were living. Thank you for your time Holson family. If there are no questions I shall leave you to talk amongst yourselves."

"I wanted to know when the sentencing court date is, and can we please attend."

"Yes, you absolutely may attend. This date will be April 11, 2017, at eight o'clock a.m. San Bernardino Superior Court, Big Bear."

"If we have any more questions for you would it be okay to contact you at the number I phoned today?"

"Yes, sir, please feel free, and thank you for all of your help. It is greatly appreciated."

"You and your family are very welcome. My deepest sympathies to you all. Thank you for your time, and hospitality, I will be on my way." We all seem to walk him to the door out of reverence and respect. All of us saying thank you at the same time, but feeling broken all over again. I knew we would all heal together again and this time not looking back. I could feel Dad's presence, I could feel his proud heart within mine somehow. I just knew he was at peace now, and so was I.

We all sat together as a family talking about what had just happened, thanking God, and reminiscing about Dad again until late that night. I knew I needed to work, but I needed this family time right here, right now, so did Lacy and Mom.

I went to work the next day feeling like a dark cloud had been lifted away from my life. I had a lot to look forward to, we all did. I called my therapist to make an appointment and she apologized for not believing me.

The Disturbed

I forgave her, I figured maybe this was her way of learning that not everyone with a disorder with side-effects of delusions is not telling the complete truth. I stayed on my meds and did amazing. I slept well, felt well, and the delusions were under control. I believe it was because my anxiety was under control. I knew I had to go on that trip to find my Lacy, but I also learned that I don't have to run to another place to manage my disorder. The disorder is only something I have to manage. It does not, nor will it ever define who I am inside.

The Beginning!

Resources

Steven W. Cohen,
MA, M.F.C.T
Individual, Marriage, Family Counseling,
Employee Relations Counseling, Mediation
9405 E. Flower St.
Bellflower, CA 90706
(714) 826-7349

Joan M Danto, L.C.S.W., B.C.D.
Child, Adolescent, Adult and family
Social Work
1400 N. Harbor Blvd., Suite 540
Fullerton, CA 92835
(714) 992-5111

WINDSTONE HEALTH SERVICES
Behavioral Health
12665 Garden Grove Blvd., Suite 714
Garden Grove, CA 92843
(714) 620-8590
www.windstonebehavioral.com

HIT HOME
1(800) HIT HOME

Suicide Prevention – Lifeline 1-800-273-TALK
www.suicidepreventionlifeline.org

NAMI
http://www.Nami.org/
Helpline: (800)950-6264
3803 N. Fairfax Dr., Suite 100
Arlington, Va 22203
(703)524-7600

Access Services L.A. County
1(800) 827-0829

ALMA family Services
(562) 801-4626

Battered Women's Hotline
1 (800) 548-2722

The Disturbed

Child, Family Services
Los Angeles County (213) 351-5602
Orange County (714) 704-8000

Rainbow House
San Pedro
(310) 548-5450

Medi-Cal Los Angeles County
1 (877) 597-4777
(310) 603-8962
1 (818) 854-4927

Medi-Cal Orange County
Cal-Optima
(714) 246-8500

Medi-Cal Accepted Psychological Services
(562) 988-1000
1 (800) 207-3333

211 for information

Some of these places may help you find help in the area in which you live.

Made in the USA
Las Vegas, NV
18 October 2023